WI
a

"R.J. Patterson does a fantastic job at keeping you engaged and interested. I look forward to more from this talented author."

*- **Aaron Patterson***
bestselling author of SWEET DREAMS

DEAD SHOT

"Small town life in southern Idaho might seem quaint and idyllic to some. But when local newspaper reporter Cal Murphy begins to uncover a series of strange deaths that are linked to a sticky spider web of deception, the lid on the peaceful town is blown wide open. Told with all the energy and bravado of an old pro, first-timer R.J. Patterson hits one out of the park his first time at bat with *Dead Shot*. It's that good."

*- **Vincent Zandri***
bestselling author of THE REMAINS

"You can tell R.J. knows what it's like to live in the newspaper world, but with *Dead Shot*, he's proven that he also can write one heck of a murder mystery."

*- **Josh Katzowitz***
NFL writer for CBSSports.com
& author of Sid Gillman: Father of the Passing Game

"Patterson has a mean streak about a mile wide and puts his two main characters through quite a horrible ride, which makes for good reading."

*- **Richard D.**, reader*

DEAD LINE

"This book kept me on the edge of my seat the whole time. I didn't really want to put it down. R.J. Patterson has hooked me. I'll be back for more."

*- **Bob Behler***
3-time Idaho broadcaster of the year
and play-by-play voice for Boise State football

"Like a John Grisham novel, from the very start I was pulled right into the story and couldn't put the book down. It was as if I personally knew and cared about what happened to each of the main characters. Every chapter ended with so much excitement and suspense I had to continue to read until I learned how it ended, even though it kept me up until 3:00 A.M.

- *Ray F.*, reader

DEAD IN THE WATER

"In Dead in the Water, R.J. Patterson accurately captures the action-packed saga of a what could be a real-life college football scandal. The sordid details will leave readers flipping through the pages as fast as a hurry-up offense."

- Mark Schlabach,
ESPN college sports columnist and
co-author of *Called to Coach*
and *Heisman: The Man Behind the Trophy*

THE WARREN OMISSIONS

"What can be more fascinating than a super high concept novel that reopens the conspiracy behind the JFK assassination while the threat of a global world war rests in the balance? With his new novel, *The Warren Omissions*, former journalist turned bestselling author R.J. Patterson proves he just might be the next worthy successor to Vince Flynn."

- *Vincent Zandri*
bestselling author of THE REMAINS

A DEADLY FORCE

A Brady Hawk novel

R.J. PATTERSON

A DEADLY FORCE
© Copyright 2019 R.J. Patterson

This novel is a work of fiction. Names, characters, places, and incidents either are the product of the author's imagination or are used fictitiously. Any resemblance to actual persons, living or dead, events, or locales is entirely coincidental.

First Print Edition 2019

All rights reserved. No part of this book may be reproduced or transmitted in any form or by any means, electronic or mechanical, including photocopying, recording, or by any information storage and retrieval system, without the written permission of the Publisher, except where permitted by law.

Cover Design by Books Covered

Published in the United States of America
Green E-Books
Boise Idaho 83713

For Jerry, a good friend
and a great American

CHAPTER 1

Dubai, UAE

BRADY HAWK SMOOTHED both lapels on his jacket and then adjusted his pocket square. Standing behind the coat check counter in the Burj Al Arab Jumeirah hotel restaurant was the perfect location to eye every guest. It was also the best place to nab Max Littleton's thumb drive full of dangerous secrets. Hawk smiled and nodded at Littleton as he entered the dining area, hoping to catch his attention.

All the intel on Littleton showed that the former Colton Industries engineer was a meticulous man as well as a creature of habit. The CIA put Littleton under surveillance several months earlier when he reportedly absconded with some of his company's top prototype weapon designs. Even worse, he planned to sell them to Russian arms dealer Andrei Orlovsky. However, instead of detaining Littleton, the agency decided to see what he would do with the information.

Littleton always checked his blazers when he entered restaurants. And he always kept his flash drive in his inside coat pocket. Several of the CIA reports highlighted how Littleton's carelessness with such a prized possession made him vulnerable, exposing his amateurism in the world of espionage. But one agent contradicted those conclusions, surmising that Littleton feared getting arrested in public with the stolen information in his possession and that checking his coat was a way to keep the device but not get caught with it.

Whether Littleton was sloppy or cautious, Hawk was positioned to take advantage of the move, ready to swap out the flash drive without the engineer suspecting anything.

"Good evening, sir," Hawk said. "May I take your coat?"

Littleton tilted his head down and peered over the top of his dark-rimmed glasses. "Not today. Thank you."

Hawk nodded and forced a smile. "Enjoy your dinner, sir."

Littleton shuffled over toward the hostess out of earshot before Hawk spoke.

"You're not gonna believe this," Hawk said into his coms. "Littleton refused to give me his coat."

"That's a first," said Tim Carson, Hawk's onsite partner from the CIA.

"It's also why we always have a plan B," said Alex, Hawk's wife and handler. "I thought you would've learned that by now."

"But plan A was so easy," Hawk said. "For once I'd like one of our ops to run smoothly."

"Where's the fun in that?" Carson asked. "Besides, if you made the simple switch, I'd be dressed in this janitor's uniform for nothing."

"Just hang tight and keep your fingers crossed," Hawk said. "If all goes well, I'll be guiding the asset in your direction momentarily."

Hawk strode over to the bar and asked for a glass of wine, suggesting that he was helping out one of the other servers. Despite a wary glance from the bartender, he poured a drink for Hawk, who promptly placed it on a tray and meandered across the room toward Littleton.

"I'm approaching the target now," Hawk said. "Wish me luck."

"If you can't land a wine glass in a man's lap, this mission is going nowhere fast," Alex said.

"I make no apologies about preferring to shoot a man from a half-mile away," Hawk said. "Clumsily tipping a drink onto an unsuspecting diner wasn't in my Navy SEAL training."

"I'd heard Navy training was getting soft these days, but I just didn't realize how much so," deadpanned Carson.

"Everyone's a comedian today, aren't they?" Hawk asked.

As he neared Littleton's table, Hawk glanced around the room to see if anyone was paying him any attention. They weren't. Satisfied that he was clear to proceed, he turned and feigned a stumble, splashing the red liquid all over Littleton's pants and white dress shirt.

Littleton shoved his chair backward with his knees as he stood. Staring slack-jawed at his drenched clothes, he tried to dab his pants with his napkin.

"I'm so sorry, sir," Hawk said. "Let me help you with that."

Littleton drew back as his eyes widened. "I think you've done enough already."

"Sir, please. I insist."

Hawk whipped out his pocket square and began mopping up the excess liquid on Littleton's pants. However, the engineer jumped back.

"Do you mind?" Littleton asked before muttering a slew of expletives.

"Let me show you to the restroom," Hawk said.

Littleton sighed and looked at his lunch guest. "I'm sorry. It'll only take a moment for me to clean this up."

The man nodded and leaned back in his chair. Meanwhile, two waiters rushed over to attend to

Hawk's mess that had attracted the attention of nearby diners.

Hawk gestured toward the restroom with an extended hand and scurried after Littleton. Embarrassed by the stain, he used his napkin to keep the spot on his shirt hidden.

When they reached the restroom, Carson was mopping the floor, appearing disinterested as he bobbed his head to the music blaring through his earbuds. Hawk flashed a faint smile at Carson who kept easing his mop across the wet ground. In the event that they had to resort to their backup plan, Carson was prepared, stocking his cart with a stain remover. Hawk hustled over to his partner and grabbed the cleaning solvent.

"Let me help you with that," Hawk said as he took the front of Littleton's shirt and sprayed the cleaner all over it. "Again, I'm so sorry, sir. I should've been more careful."

Littleton stopped and studied Hawk closely. "Is that a Texas accent I detect in your voice?"

Hawk nodded and held up his right hand as if he was being sworn in. "Guilty as charged. American by birth, Texan by the grace of God."

Littleton chuckled at the response. "Nice to hear a familiar accent over here. We Texans need to stick together."

Hawk nodded. "No question about that. Where are you from? East Texas? West Texas? God forbid one of those sprawling metropolises that's just ruining our great state."

Littleton shrugged. "Houston, though I grew up just outside of Lubbock."

"So, you're not a transplant?"

"Born and raised," Littleton said. "I only leave the state to deal with pressing business matters. Regardless of where I go in the world, my mind is always back home in the Lone Star state. It'd be foolish to live anywhere else."

Hawk extended his hands toward Littleton's coat. "Let me take that for you and see if I can clean it up. I saw a little bit splash on the sleeves there."

"Sure," Littleton said, his tone sufficiently softened by their connection. He handed his jacket to Hawk, who wasted no time in slipping his hand inside Littleton's coat pocket and palming the device.

Carson eased past them and snatched the flash drive from Hawk's hand. Hawk shot him a knowing glance before Carson disappeared into the far corner of the room.

While Hawk would've scrubbed furiously if his intent had been to remove the stain, he worked his way methodically across the sleeve with his rag in order to give Carson enough time.

"How's it coming, Carson?" Alex asked over the coms.

"I'm having a little trouble cracking the encryption on this thing," Carson whispered.

"We don't have much time, so hurry it up, will ya?"

Hawk listened to the banter in his ear and wished Alex had been able to accompany him on the trip. However, due to the nature of the mission, Carson was chosen because of his computer wizardry. And being a man in a Muslim country also contributed to the decision to pass over Alex.

Come on, come on. I can't stall forever.

"This shirt almost looks spotless," Littleton said. "Just a faint stain here. It won't save the shirt, but at least I won't be embarrassed the rest of the day."

Hawk stopped what he was doing and peered at Littleton's work. "Nice job. Maybe you can show me how to work such magic on this sleeve. I'm not making as much headway as you did."

Littleton frowned as he looked over the top of his glasses and surveyed the spot on the sleeve. "No need to be so ornery," he said, directing the comment at his coat.

Without hesitating, Littleton dipped his rag beneath the water and went to work.

"Looks like you've almost got it," Hawk said, encouraging Littleton while simultaneously alerting Carson that time was almost up.

"Carson?" Alex said. "Where are you at with this thing?"

Carson sighed. "I'm still having trouble with—"

After a moment of silence, Alex sought answers. "What is it?" she asked.

"I just got in," he said. "Give me a minute."

"I don't think you've got a minute."

Hawk cringed as he listened to the news. Carson had told him that he needed at least a minute to download the designs from the flash drive and upload dummy files as well as a faux encryption key. And based on how Littleton was moving, Carson was going to have thirty seconds at best.

Littleton held up his coat and studied the sleeves for a moment. "Now no one will think I'm a slob."

"That's always a good thing," Hawk said. "It definitely increases your chances with the ladies. They like men who are put together."

Littleton shook his head. "Never had much luck with the ladies no matter how neat I am. Perhaps if I knew how to carry on a conversation without stumbling over my words, I might get a second date once in a while."

Hawk smiled. "Again, sir, I'm incredibly sorry about all this."

Littleton slapped Hawk on his shoulder. "Don't worry about it. I'll survive the rest of the day, and no one will be the wiser."

"You're probably right, sir," Hawk said as he watched the engineer slip into his coat.

Littleton inspected his coat once more and then strode toward the door—and the flash drive was still nowhere to be seen.

"Almost there," Carson said into the coms. "Stall him for ten more seconds, Hawk."

"Sir, just a moment," Hawk said as he walked across the room after Littleton. "You forgot something."

Littleton placed his hand on the door before stopping and turning. "What is it, Tex?"

Hawk's mind went into overdrive as he tried to concoct a reason to stop Littleton from exiting the restroom.

"Your pocket square, sir," Hawk said. "It's a little crooked."

Carson flushed the toilet and emerged from the stall. He seamlessly slipped the device into Hawk's hand, which he held behind his back.

Then Hawk approached Littleton and stood eye to eye with the engineer before taking his jacket by the lapels and easing the flash drive back into the coat pocket. Hawk pulled Littleton's blazer taut before brushing off a piece of lint on his right shoulder.

"Now you'll be able to survive the day—and

maybe get a second date, too, if you so wish," Hawk said.

"Thanks," Littleton said before he spun and exited.

When the door fell shut, Hawk exhaled and turned toward Carson. "What the hell was that?"

"You thought plan B was going to run smoothly after our first idea bombed?" Carson asked.

"I never anticipate everything going as planned, but I thought they brought you on because you were some computer genius and could crack any encryption in a matter of seconds."

"Perhaps my skills were oversold a little bit."

Hawk shook his head. "That almost cost us this operation. And we can't be setting off alarm bells when we're in this deep."

"Just relax, will ya? It all worked out."

Hawk set his jaw and clenched his fist. For a moment, he contemplated punching Carson.

"Do better next time," Hawk said. "We don't have the margins to be screwing around here. Every other scenario that could've happened would've torpedoed this mission, especially our chances of digging deeper into what Orlovsky is up to."

While Hawk and Alex had earlier retrieved a list of clients from Orlovsky's computer, specific information about who exactly some of the people were and how to contact them were unclear. However, the CIA recognized they had an opportunity to embed a virus onto Orlovsky's computer that would create backdoor access. Hawk pleaded with Phoenix Foundation director J.D. Blunt to let Alex join them, but he deferred to the CIA, who had assumed command of the operation. With Carson's near flub, Hawk hoped that would be worthy ammunition to convince the agency that his wife was the best operative with extraordinary skills when it came to computers and various other forms of electronics.

Carson met Hawk's gaze and locked there for a moment. Nothing was said, but it was clear that the CIA's darling didn't like getting called out for sloppy work.

"Let's get upstairs," Carson said. "They're going to make the exchange soon if everything is going well."

Hawk followed Carson out of the restroom and down a long hallway before taking the stairwell up to the fifth floor. Once they entered their room and shut the door, Carson held up his index finger, signaling for Hawk to be silent. Carson walked across the room and picked up a gray box about the size of a matchbox and flipped a switch.

"Please speak freely," Carson said.

"I thought I already was," Hawk fired back.

"Look, I get it. I know you're upset that we barely were able to get the device back into Littleton's pocket in time, but we did," Carson said. "So just chill out. I may not have been your first choice, but we got the job done."

"It's not over yet," Hawk said as he settled onto the foot of the bed in front of several monitors that Carson set up on the dresser. "Littleton still has to go through with it. And I'm not sure he has the stomach for it."

Carson raised his eyebrows. "You get a soft spot for that traitor all of a sudden just because he said some nice things about Texas?"

"Just call it a hunch," Hawk said. "But even if he does go through with it, he should be easy to extract all the necessary information from once you capture him."

"It's your job to capture him," Carson said with a snarl.

"My job is to make sure you don't screw up again. Now, once this transaction is over, I'm going out. And I expect you to snatch Littleton to ensure he doesn't get away."

"You're going to just abandon me here?" Carson asked, his voice sliding up an octave every few words.

"We discussed this earlier," Hawk said. "I have somewhere to be."

"Does your wife know about this?" Carson asked. "I can just turn our coms back on."

Hawk wagged his index finger at Carson. "You might get to call the shots when you're with the agency, but not here. I suggest you shut your mouth if you know what's good for you."

The two men sat in silence for the next fifteen minutes while Carson pounded out a few commands on his keyboard. The monitors came to life, showing an empty hotel room.

"Are you sure they're going to make the exchange here?" Carson asked.

Hawk nodded. "That's the intelligence we received."

"I hope it's right. Otherwise, we're screwed."

"Just keep watching. He'll be there."

While posing as a member of the hotel staff, Hawk discovered what room Carson's contact was staying in, which was the room next door to Orlovsky. After gaining access, Hawk had used some of the CIA's most advanced surveillance technology to set up undetectable cameras everywhere.

"Let's bring Alex back in on this and see if she can be of any assistance," Carson said.

Hawk didn't mind. In fact, he preferred that someone else be listening to the kind of inane banter emanating from Carson's mouth.

After another tense minute, Hawk and Carson watched as the door opened on the screen and Littleton trudged through with Orlovsky's associate. The man sat down at the desk and fired up his computer. Hawk watched intently as Littleton went through the protocol of exchanging passwords and routing numbers in order to hand over the information.

"He could type in utter gibberish and that file would still open," Alex said over the coms.

"Excellent work," Hawk said, acknowledging her assistance in putting together the files used to create the flash drive with all the fake information.

The man dialed a number on his cell phone and put it on speaker.

"Mr. Orlovsky, we have the package," the man said.

"Excellent. Can you verify its authenticity?" Orlovsky's voice boomed over the speaker.

"Just give me a minute," the man said. "I'm almost there."

Hawk and Carson didn't move, their eyes fixated on the screen as they watched the unfolding scene.

"Got it," the man said. "Checking now, but it looks fine to me."

"Wire him the funds and thank him," Orlovsky said.

"Of course," the man said.

Carson sighed and looked at Hawk. "They're going to kill Littleton."

"We need to get him out of there right now," Hawk said.

"Got any ideas?" Carson asked.

"Everybody got what they wanted," Hawk said. "I suggest we use a time-tested method."

Without hesitating, he raced into the hallway and yanked the fire alarm. While in the U.S., such a stunt would draw little more than a raised eyebrow, but in Dubai, the sound sent all the foreign guests into a frenzy. In a matter of a seconds, people spilled into the hallways and scrambled toward the stairwells to exit the building.

Hawk shrugged as he returned to the room. "Are they still there?"

"For now," Carson said, "but it looks like they're about to leave."

"They're on the sixth floor, right?" Hawk asked. Carson nodded.

"Then you better get up there in a hurry," Hawk said. "Orlovsky's man would make me, and that would blow the whole op."

Carson ripped off his janitor overalls and raced out the door.

Hawk followed his colleague but headed in the opposite direction.

"What's going on now?" Alex asked.

"I'm leaving," Hawk said. "Carson can handle this on his own."

"Maybe you should stick around," she said.

"I'm having . . . time . . . you," Hawk said, feigning a bad connection.

"You're breaking up on me, Hawk. Say that again."

"Craziness . . . hotel . . . go."

"Say that again."

Hawk turned off his coms and headed downstairs. He didn't want Alex to know what he was about to do.

CHAPTER 2

Hong Kong

TITUS BLACK STOOD STILL amidst the tsunami of people speed walking along the sidewalk. He couldn't imagine living in a metropolis where every day was a fight just to navigate through the bustling crowds. If he was going to fight, he preferred the hand-to-hand combat variety. He didn't mind using weapons either. But today, his weapon was a small cardboard box.

After a deep breath, he plunged into the stream of workers scurrying to their place of employment. According to the address given to him, General Fortner was holed up in a low-frills condo approximately three blocks away. Black had studied pictures from the building's website, which tried to woo ex-pats with its reasonable prices and pristine views. He needed to be familiar with the layout in case Fortner decide to run. Not that the old Navy commander stood a chance in a footrace against Black.

Sporting a hat, sunglasses, and brown UPS jacket, Black reached the lobby in five minutes and stopped to survey the fifty-seven-story structure soaring over him. He waited until a gentleman toting a briefcase punched in his access code to open the door. Slipping casually behind him, Black headed toward the stairwell, opting to stay away from any security cameras and avoiding any potential residents who might be able to identify him if the situation went south. Fortner had proven to be a worthy adversary, always prepared and seemingly one step ahead of Black's best-laid plans.

When Black reached the nineteenth floor, he entered the long corridor and strode toward Fortner's condo located in the far corner. Black pulled out his weapon and knocked on the door, hiding his gun beneath the box. After a couple more knocks, Black didn't hear any stirring inside and wondered if he was standing at the right door. He confirmed that he was and decided to knock one last time.

After he pounded again, the door next to Fortner's condo swung open, and an elderly gentleman shuffled out with a cane. He spoke in a crisp American accent, immediately indicating that the man was also an ex-pat.

"All that racket isn't necessary, you know," the man said. "If he wanted to open the door, he would. Just leave the package downstairs like you're supposed to."

Black shrugged. "I need for the recipient to sign for this."

"We have a protocol for this so we don't have delivery men combing the halls of our condo every minute of the day. You must be new."

"What gave it away?" Black asked.

"Well, for starters you don't look like the guy I saw in the lobby last week."

"Guilty as charged."

"But that's not all."

"What else makes me look like a rookie?" Black asked.

The old man raised his cane and pointed it at the box. "This has nothing to do with you being a rookie, but you're hiding something under there."

"Under where?"

"Under that box," the man said. "And I suspect it isn't a clipboard holding papers for the general to sign."

"You know the man who lives here?" Black asked, ignoring the man's accusation.

"Who are you with? CIA? Navy SEALs? Army Rangers?"

Black eyed the man closely. "Who are you?"

The old man hobbled near Black and offered his hand. "James McCutcheon, retired FBI."

Black shifted the gun from his right hand to his left, keeping the weapon out of sight, before shaking but not revealing his identity.

"I'm the one who reported that an Army general was living here—and up to no good," McCutcheon said. "They didn't tell you about me?"

Black shook his head.

"Well, that's comforting, I guess," McCutcheon said. "They at least took me serious and sent someone."

"Since it looks like the general isn't here, what else can you tell me about him?" Black asked.

"I know he's involved in some activities he shouldn't be, the kind that get you killed if you're not careful."

"That should be the least of his concerns," Black said. "He's on the run for good reason."

"All I know is that over the past few weeks, I've seen guys here from a local gang that's known for its involvement in fixing soccer matches. Gambling is a big problem in Hong Kong as you might well imagine. A bunch of retired people with loads of expendable income looking for ways to spend it and do so in a way that's entertaining."

"Do you know where these shady characters hang out?" Black asked.

"They're part of a gang known as Long Zi. From what I've heard, they have a place down at the docks. It's how they get their illegal money in and out of the country. If you ask around, someone will point you in the right direction."

"I appreciate your help and your continued service to your country," Black said. "Hopefully we'll be able to find the general soon and bring him to justice."

"What did he do, if you don't mind me asking?"

Black eyed the man carefully. "He's done enough to warrant some agency sending me halfway across the world to look for him and take him back to Washington."

"Good luck catching your man."

Black watched McCutcheon return to his condo and shut the door behind him before a series of six clicks echoed in the hallway, presumably from all the deadbolts he used as a safety measure. While Black didn't want to admit it, he recognized that he saw a possible glimpse into his future in McCutcheon: old, tired, and paranoid, living in a foreign country and wanting to disappear.

Black dismissed the thought as he eased back into the stairwell and headed toward the docks.

McCutcheon might have been old, but his instincts were still sharp as a tack. However, Black wondered why McCutcheon was never mentioned in the official report given to the Phoenix Foundation.

The fifteen-minute walk down the docks gave Black time to think about how he might approach his inquiry into Fortner's whereabouts. It'd have to be handled delicately, especially since no one even knew Black's itinerary. Blunt's orders specified that Black not communicate with the team until Fortner was in custody. And Black didn't argue, given how likely it was that Fortner had someone at the Pentagon and CIA feeding him information on the agency's approach to apprehending him. Before leaving for Hong Kong, even the mission prep meeting with Blunt was held offsite just to ensure that someone hadn't planted an undetectable bug in the conference room.

When Black reached the docks, he asked a couple workers where he might be able to find Long Zi. After several scowls without even a word uttered, Black wondered if should continue his search or set up surveillance on Fortner's condo instead. Black was almost resigned to a stake out when he was approached by a worker.

"I hear you are looking for Long Zi," the man said.

Black nodded. "That's right. Do you know how to find them?"

"They're not the kind of people you want to deal with. Trust me. You're better off leaving and keeping your mouth shut if you know what's best for you."

"Let's just say that I don't know what's best for me," Black said. "Could you at least point me in the right direction?"

The man sighed. "If you're that stupid, just don't say I didn't warn you when they're beating you senseless."

"That's not going to happen."

The man chuckled. "If you say so. Now, if you're that determined to find Long Zi, they'll be at dock number seventy-eight. But don't expect to find anyone there before ten o'clock at night. Because of the nature of what they do, the daylight isn't the best time for them to conduct their business."

"Thank you for your help, sir."

"You may thank me now, but I doubt you'll thank me later," the man said before he spun on his heels and walked away.

Black smiled. He couldn't wait to find Fortner.

* * *

JUST AFTER 10:30 P.M., Black approached Long Zi's office located at dock number twenty-seven. He gnawed on a toothpick, turning it around in his mouth before knocking on the door. After half a minute, a towering burly man sporting a tank top to show off a variety of tattoos on his rippling biceps answered.

"We're not available," the man said as he tried to slam the door.

Black had planted his foot inside.

"You'll move your foot if you know what's good for you," the man said with a snarl.

"Not until you tell me where General Fortner is," Black said.

"Who?"

"The American general," Black said. "You know who I'm talking about."

"No, I don't. And I'm not going to ask you again to move."

Black peered behind the man and noticed several tables with stacks of money being counted by various workers. Not a single one of them even looked in Black's direction, intently focused on their task.

With a swift move, the man punched Black in the stock. However, Black was able to get his hands in a defensive position to soften the blow. Then he unleashed several hits on the man, first up high and then down low. Saving the throat for the final flurry of punches, Black drew back and regretted that he didn't deliver the hit sooner. The man kicked Black in his knees, sending him staggering backward onto the docks. Black stumbled over a pile of ropes and nearly lost his balance.

Once he regained his footing, Black rocked back and forth before exploding into a sprint toward the man. However, Black never made it as he was blindsided by another one of Long Zi's gang members.

Black fell to the ground, his face pressed against the wooden planks by the tattooed giant. Meanwhile, Black was forced to endure a relentless barrage of kicks from the gangsters who had swarmed around him. He counted at least a half dozen different people before he could no longer keep his eyes open.

Mercifully, the beating finally stopped less than a minute later, though Black would've sworn it went on for fifteen.

"Maybe next time you'll listen when someone tells you to leave," the giant said as he yanked Black to his feet. "Now if I ever see you around here again, I won't make the boys stop until you're dead. Do you understand me?"

Black nodded and moaned before getting shoved backward. He couldn't maintain his balance and tumbled to the ground. As Black tried to sit up, he heard uproarious laughter followed by the door slamming. He remained still for a few minutes before contemplating standing.

I should've listened to McCutcheon.

Black finally staggered to his feet and left the docks. He kept his head down, certain that he would scare any small children—or anyone else—who happened to be out at this hour of night. Struggling to walk in a straight line, Black stopped, fearful that he might draw the attention of any Hong Kong police officers patrolling the streets as being publicly intoxicated. After resting on a bench for a spell, he decided he was strong enough to make the short walk back to his hotel. But before he could get going, a woman rushed over to him.

"Sir, are you okay?" she asked, kneeling next to Black.

Black held up his hand. "I'm fine, I'm fine. No need to worry."

"You're not fine," she said, her eyes scanning his beaten body. "Who did this to you? Was it someone in Long Zi?"

"Look, I appreciate your concern, but I don't need your help," Black said. "I was just taking a short break, and I'll be able to address these wounds when I get back to my place."

"I doubt that," she said as she stood and remained there, hovering over him. "You need professional medical help."

"Your concern is certainly kind, but I'm not

going to a hospital," Black said.

"Who said anything about going to a hospital?" she asked. "I'm a nurse, and a damn good one. Come with me, and I'll get you fixed up."

Black groaned as he eased upright. He grabbed his back and shuffled with the woman down the sidewalk.

"You don't have to do this, you know," Black said.

"Nonsense," she said. "You need some medical care, and if you're being foolish enough not to visit an emergency room, I'll help you. My apartment is just up ahead."

When they reached her apartment, she assisted Black inside and helped him over to the couch. "Just lie down there. I'll be right back."

She returned with a first aid kit along with a couple ice packs and a cup.

"Drink this," she said, handing Black a glass of water. "And then put your head back so I can start dressing these wounds."

Black complied and then unbuttoned his shirt with the woman's help. "I have a hard fast rule that I don't let women take my shirt off without knowing their name first."

"Some rules are made to be broken," she said with a wry smile.

"My name is Titus," he said.

"I'm Liling. It's a pleasure to meet you, Titus, though I would've preferred different circumstances."

"Me and you both," he said as he removed his shirt. "Do you always go around helping random strangers on the street and inviting them into your apartment to give them medical attention?"

"Only when the situation calls for it. Most of the time, people call me instead."

"You make in-home visits?"

She nodded. "Many of the ex-pats here are afraid of visiting our hospitals unless they absolutely have to. So, I go and determine if what they're feeling demands further care or if they just need to suck it up and pop a couple aspirin."

"And you only deal with ex-pats?"

She nodded. "They pay far more than my fellow countrymen, and I get to practice my English."

Black's eyes widened. "You don't sound like you need to practice English. In fact, if I didn't know any better, I would've thought you attended school in the U.S. Your pronunciations are flawless."

"I've had a little help from one client in particular," she said. "I think he was a general in your army."

She laughed softly as she poured some anti-septic onto a cut on his side. "Well, that's what he told me, at least. I'm not sure if some of these old men are lying just to try to impress me."

Black reached into his pocket and pulled out his phone. He quickly swiped to a picture of Fortner. "He didn't happen to look like this, did he?"

Liling leaned over and peered at the image for a second. "That's him all right. You must know him."

"I'm looking for him, and apparently he has some less than hospitable friends down at the docks."

"I would've never helped him if I knew that," she said.

"Well, apparently he's not at his home or at the docks, at least from what I could see tonight before I got beaten. Got any ideas as to where he might be?"

Liling took a deep breath and stared at the ceiling. "He was always so drunk that I never knew if he was telling the truth or not, but he did talk about how he loved to go to his place in New Orleans. He said he loved Mardi Gras and partying on Bourbon Street."

Black glanced at the date on his phone. "Mardi Gras starts next week."

"Maybe that's why you haven't been able to find him."

"I have to start looking somewhere."

CHAPTER 3

Dubai, UAE

HAWK INSERTED ANOTHER earbud and turned it on as he exited the Burj Al Arab Jumeirah hotel. Amidst the chaotic scene of everyone fleeing, Hawk hailed a taxi and gave the driver directions to a restaurant three miles away. Once they reached the destination, Hawk paid the man and got out.

"Are you in your office?" Hawk asked over the coms.

"Affirmative," Blunt said.

"I just want to state for the record that I don't like doing this," Hawk said. "Keeping secrets from Alex is something I loathe."

"That's only the seventh time you've gone on record as saying that during this trip," Blunt said. "I think that fact is abundantly clear now. But the truth is, you're both spies and you'll always have *some* secrets that must be kept from each other."

Hawk held up his phone and acted as if he was talking on it. He detested people who walked around with Bluetooth ear buds and carried on conversations like it was normal. Despite doing it often on missions, Hawk wanted to avoid the appearance of looking like Mr. Businessman who acted as if he was cooler than everyone else because he was on an important phone call.

"I don't have to like it," Hawk said.

Blunt chuckled. "After a while, secrets become burdensome. They're also lucrative, which is why you're over there in the first place—to make sure Littleton doesn't fork over secrets just so he can cash in with a big payday."

"I still think you're being overcautious in keeping Alex in the dark on this," Hawk said as he walked into the lobby and waited for the elevator. "She's loyal to her country over her family."

"That's an assumption you shouldn't make."

"I hope she'd choose me over country," Hawk said.

"That's not what she signed up for—and you either," Blunt said.

"It's hard to go against human nature."

"But that's why you're such a good agent, Hawk. You defy natural instincts and do what's best for the mission and your team, holding it all in light of what's the right thing to do in terms of national security. Don't ever change."

"I don't think you'd let me," Hawk cracked as the elevator doors swung open and he stepped inside alone.

Hawk hit the button for the terrace. That was the supposed location of the meeting between Andrei Orlovsky and Shane Samuels, Alex's half brother.

"Good luck, Hawk," Blunt said.

Hawk reached into his pocket and applied the mustache to his face. Next, he put on a pair of dark sunglasses. Upon entering the restaurant, he requested a newspaper and scanned the room for Orlovsky and Samuels. They were seated in the far corner up against the large plate-glass window overlooking the water. Hawk asked to be seated in the opposite corner against the wall.

Once Hawk was situated, he turned on his directional mic. He placed it stealthily between the paper, which was positioned on the edge of the table and aimed toward the two men.

Tying the audio feed into the coms, Blunt listened in as Orlovsky and Samuels exchanged pleasantries and talked about inane things like the weather and recent sporting events.

"What does Samuels look like?" Blunt asked.

Hawk watched as the man who had once served

with the old Firestorm team dined with one of the most notorious arms dealers in the world. Samuels shifted in his seat, constantly checking over his shoulders. He had already downed one glass of what appeared to be bourbon in the short time since Hawk started observing. Perhaps as a nervous tic, Samuels dabbed the corner of his mouth after every pull on his glass.

"He looks jumpy to me," Hawk said, holding his phone up to his ear again. "He keeps looking around the room as if he's expecting someone to arrive."

Blunt chuckled. "He's waiting for you."

"I could give him what he's looking for and just toss the traitorous bastard through the window," Hawk said.

"Hawk, simmer down. You're only on an intel-gathering mission. We're just fortunate that this is going on at the same time as Littleton's shenanigans."

"Two birds, one stone," Hawk said. "That's the J.D. Blunt way."

"Efficiency is a highly underrated skill. That's why we can do so much with so little."

"Are you trying to make me mad with that insult?"

Blunt grunted. "Since when did you become such a snowflake, Hawk?"

"When I found out it grates on your nerves,"

Hawk said with a grin.

"You're smiling right now, aren't you?"

"Can you hear it in my voice?"

"One day I'm going to hurl one of those bourbon bottles you get me right back at you."

Hawk laughed softly. "I'll be getting you alcohol served only in soft wineskins from now on."

When the waiter returned with another drink for Samuels, Hawk sat up in his seat. "I know good and well that these two didn't come here to talk about sports and the weather. This ought to get interesting if Samuels can stay sober."

Hawk focused again on the conversation happening just across the room.

"I think you can provide me with a valuable service," Orlovsky said. "I'm missing an entire piece of the market due to Americans' reluctance to purchase these weapons. The seeds of chaos are sown by men determined to see change and who expect to reap a harvest of peace."

"If you replace the word *peace* with *power*, you might have just nailed what most of those groups are really about," Samuels said.

"And you and I will reap the greatest rewards available—financial prosperity."

"I'm not looking to get rich," Samuels said. "I'm looking to disappear forever."

"That's something you can only do with enough money. And you're going to need lots of it, my friend."

"I'm confident that I can work with these groups to purchase your products. However, I want to make sure there are no ties to me. Can you assure me that I won't be linked to your operation?"

"Of course," Orlovsky said. "We try to keep our digital footprint to a minimum, so in the unlikely event that someone does steal information from us, they're not going to end up with anything valuable. I have a decryption key that keeps most everything neat and tidy."

"I do have one final question," Samuels said.

Orlovsky gestured for his new potential business partner to continue. "Go ahead. Better to get it all out now."

"How do you intend to get these weapons into the country without being detected? Our ports are some of the most strenuously patrolled in the world."

Orlovsky laughed. "There are far more efficient ways to sneak weapons into a country than using freighters. But don't you worry about that. You get the clients to part with their money and leave the logistics me."

"It looks like I'll have to trust your judgment," Samuels said.

Orlovsky smiled and opened his arms wide. "I'm still here, aren't I? If the CIA could eliminate me, I'm sure they would've by now."

Hawk stifled a snicker. "Are you getting all this, Blunt?"

"Loud and clear. That asshole has no idea that we're using him to remove all his clients one by one."

"I like how this is playing out," Hawk said.

He watched as the two men returned to their banal banter once their food arrived. However, just when Hawk didn't think anything else interesting was going to be said, Samuels wiped his hands on his napkin and leaned back in his chair.

"I know some potential targets if any of your clients are searching for some," Samuels said.

"Looking to make a little extra money?" Orlovsky asked. "What do you Americans call that? A side hustle, is it?"

Samuels laughed. "We all must do what we can to make ends meet."

"If you're able to secure clients for me, you won't have any problems paying all of your bills and then some."

The waiter drifted by and asked them if they wanted any dessert before leaving the check. Orlovsky took the bill and slapped several bills on top of it before rising.

"I will be in touch," Samuels said.

"I look forward to working with you," Orlovsky said.

With that parting comment, the Russian arms dealer strode toward the exit and then pocketed a handful of chocolate mints from the hostess stand on his way to the foyer.

"They're all wrapped up," Hawk said. "Want me to nab this traitorous piece of garbage? I could beat some sense into him."

"Leave him alone, Hawk," Blunt said. "We found out what we needed to know."

"Did we? He was spying on Firestorm, and now he's offering to give up target information to Orlovsky. You know he's talking about us."

"But he doesn't know where we are now," Blunt said.

"Can you be sure of that?"

"Can you be sure that he does?" Blunt fired back. "We need to let this play out. If Samuels is going to contact Orlovsky on a regular basis, we'll have a much better way of keeping tabs on all his illegal activity than if we simply bring in Samuels."

"He betrayed all of us," Hawk said.

"That's part of the job. Don't let it affect your overall mission."

"We brought him in like he was family—and we

later found out he was. But then we learned he was spying on us. And we've never been given an explanation why. It's an unforgivable offense."

"Just stay focused, Hawk. No one is ever straightforward with you in our business."

"Doesn't matter. He was Alex's half brother, and now he's threatening to give up our location to anyone who wants to attack us."

"Simmer down. Once we're done using Samuels, I'll let you bring him in and ask him all the questions you'd like to ask. Just get back to Carson and help him."

"He doesn't need me. Carson can handle Littleton on his own."

"Hawk," Blunt said, drawing out the name as his voice went higher, "I'm warning you to leave Samuels alone. We've already got our hands full."

Hawk didn't say a word. He set his jaw as he watched Samuels walk out of the restaurant. But Hawk was determined not to let the former operative get too far.

"Hawk, are you still there?" Blunt asked.

Still silence.

"Hawk, don't be screwing around on this one. Leave him a—"

Hawk turned off his earbud and followed Samuels out of the restaurant.

Staying far enough back not to get made, Hawk used the people milling around in the lobby as a sufficient cover. His disguise likely would've sufficed, but he didn't want to take any chances, especially since Blunt was adamant about leaving Samuels alone.

Hawk watched as Samuels slid into a dark sedan that sped away. Searching for a cab, Hawk was shut down when he was directed to the back of the line by the concierge at a taxi stand. Unable to go any farther, he put his earbud back in and tried to reach Blunt over the coms.

"You still there?" Hawk asked.

"I swear if you have Samuels—"

"Don't get your knickers in a knot. He's gone and didn't see me."

"Get your ass back to Washington, pronto," Blunt said. "We've got more important matters to attend to than your personal vendettas."

CHAPTER 4

Washington, D.C.

BLUNT PINCHED THE BRIDGE of his nose as he gnawed on his unlit cigar. He'd been poring over a series of files received earlier that morning and was awaiting the arrival of his team to discuss next steps in the multiple operations the Phoenix Foundation was running. In the two days since Hawk and Black were both in the field, Blunt had amassed a treasure trove of intel related to a hunch he was chasing down related to Obsidian.

Alex appeared in the conference room, sporting a flowing navy-blue dress with her hair tightly cropped in a bun. She whistled a tune that Blunt couldn't place but was sure he'd heard before.

"What song is that?" Blunt asked.

"I doubt you've ever heard it."

"Try me."

"*Pehli Baar Dil Ye* from the Bollywood film 'Hum

Ho Gaye Aap Ke'.'"

Blunt stared at her blankly. "You're right. I've never heard of it, never seen it, never will."

"Not enough things blowing up for you?"

Blunt chuckled. "I know you think that I live to make things explode, but I enjoy period drama pieces too."

Alex's eyes widened. "Period drama pieces? You?"

"Yeah, dramas from periods of war like 'Tora, Tora, Tora' and 'Enola Gay' and 'The Dirty Dozen'."

"Might I suggest you broaden your horizons sometime?" she asked. "Hawk and I have an extensive collection of Bollywood films."

"I'll pass. I can't read subtitled movies. Makes my head hurt."

"We have a few that are dubbed," she said with a wry grin.

"Hard pass on that one too. Those Kung Fu movies where everybody's mouth is out of sync make me want to punch somebody."

Black strolled into the room and settled into the seat across from Alex.

"So, what rousing conversation am I missing out on?" he asked.

"I'm trying to convince Blunt to expand his movie tastes, and he seems dead set against it."

Black shrugged. "If you're pedaling those Bollywood films again, I don't blame him."

"And what's wrong with appreciating another culture's film offerings?"

"Because they're crap, that's why."

Hawk shut the door behind him as he settled next to Alex. "What's crap?"

"Bollywood films," Blunt said. "I'd rather have my eyes taped open and be forced to watch that Ben Affleck disaster *Gigli* for twenty-four hours straight than watch fifteen minutes of a Bollywood flick."

"Harsh," Hawk said. "Though I thoroughly enjoyed Ben Affleck's *Argo*, despite it resembling somewhat of a normal workday around here."

"Well, speaking of work, let's get to it," Blunt said. "Lord knows we've got more terrorists crawling out from underneath rocks than we can shake a stick at it."

"All trying to get a piece of Orlovsky's latest new technology, ripped off straight from Colton Industries?" Black asked.

"He certainly must've advertised the fact that he was getting some innovative designs from a major weapons company," Alex said. "But thanks to Hawk and his new friend from the CIA, Orlovsky's got nothing of substance."

"And what about Littleton?" Black asked.

"We're detaining him for now," Blunt said. "And when the time comes, I might let you interrogate him."

"I think what we all want to know is if that backdoor we planted on the flash drive helped us connect the dots between Orlovsky and any Obsidian operatives," Hawk said.

"And the answer to that is a big fat *maybe*," Alex said. "Since our database on who is involved with Obsidian is still relatively short, it's difficult to tell. At this point, all I can say is that Orlovsky is only partial to money. If you've got it, you can be his client."

"We need to keep digging into that," Blunt said, nodding at Alex. "I'm sure there are more avenues to explore since we've been able to get into his mainframe."

Alex shifted in her seat and sat up straight. "I'm still rummaging through every piece of data I can find on his machine. So far, I've found nothing definitive, but I'm not giving up yet, so don't you worry."

"That's my Alex," Blunt said before grunting. "Like a dog with a bone."

"Speaking of dogs, I need to update the team about General Fortner," Black said.

Hawk shook his head. "Please tell me you're about to show us photos of the bullet you put in his head."

"I'd never let that traitor off that easily," Black

said. "Besides, we have big plans to use him to climb the ladder with Obsidian and find out who's calling the shots."

"So, what did you find?" Hawk asked.

Black pushed a folder across the table toward Hawk. "Fortner has a place on Bourbon Street in New Orleans that he's apparently living in these days."

"If you need help flushing him out any time soon, just let me know," Hawk said. "I'd be more than happy to assist you."

Blunt raised his hands. "We'll consider that as well, but we can't lose any more leads. We need concrete connections to Obsidian's upper brass. And I think we might just have one."

Hawk leaned forward, his elbows resting on the table. "Where'd you dig this one up?"

"Perfect choice of words, Hawk," Blunt said with a grin. "It all started with an obituary."

"Who died?" Alex asked.

"Nancy Coleman, the filthy rich New York socialite," Blunt said.

"Are we supposed to know who she is?" Black asked. "If she was on one of those reality shows, I sure as hell have never seen her or know anything about her."

Blunt shook his head. "No, she wasn't one to step into the limelight, other than her one major indiscretion, which was having an affair with married U.S. Senator Richard Antley."

"That was all over the news," Alex said. "I'd almost forgotten the woman who was involved with him."

"Yeah, well I didn't," Blunt said. "Turns out, Antley blabbed about Firestorm to Nancy and not-so-subtly urged her to talk with one of her journalist friends about it. Nancy's daughter just so happened to go to college with Camille Youngblood."

"Now that's a name I'll never forget," Alex said.

"Me either," Blunt said. "Though we shut down Firestorm before Camille wrote anything about us, starting over has been a pain in the ass. And I never forget those who cause such pain."

Hawk chuckled.

"What's so funny?" Blunt asked.

"You've built a team of people who all cause you varying degrees of pain each day," Hawk said. "I'm starting to wonder if you're a masochist."

"That's what it feels like sometimes," Blunt said. "Now, Coleman's death wasn't anything I celebrated, but her obituary had a bit of information that I took a keen interest in."

"Inheritance issues?" Black asked.

Blunt shrugged. "In a sense, yes. It wasn't anything crazy like a Grisham novel where everybody's scrapping over a five billion dollar inheritance. Nancy didn't have any children. However, she was quite a prolific philanthropist and chose to leave her entire fortune to just one non-profit called A Hand Up."

"A Hand Up," Alex said, furrowing her brow. "I've never heard of them."

"Neither had I," Blunt said, "but they're no small player. According to their website, they have offices all over the world in places like Paris, Geneva, London, Frankfurt, Madrid, Chicago, and New York."

"Impressive," Hawk said.

"That's what I thought," Blunt said. "But then I started digging through news articles about them. And you know what I found?"

All three of Blunt's employees shook their heads.

"Nothing," Blunt said, answering his own question. "It was like A Hand Up didn't even exist. At first, I thought this was an obvious front, but they have legitimate offices in all those countries and supposedly do good work according to one watchdog website. However, the people heading each one of those branches gave me reason to pause and consider what might be going on."

Blunt stood and paced around the room as he continued.

"Each branch had ties to a prominent financial guru in each of those countries," he said. "So, I called in a few favors with one of my friends at the NSA and asked him to compile a dossier about each one of those men. And what he found was something that reaffirmed my suspicions."

"What was that?" Alex asked.

"Each one of those men made a fortune on the stock market on days coinciding with different tragic events worldwide," Blunt said. "It's almost as if they all knew about it in advance and adjusted their portfolios accordingly."

"Want me to delve deeper into this guy running the New York City branch?" Alex asked.

Blunt shook his head. "I want you and Hawk to go there and investigate on site. Hack their financials and find out what's going on."

She nodded. "Sounds better than the last time we went there to diffuse a dirty nuke."

"Just think of it like this," Blunt said. "Your last trip made this trip possible."

"And are you sending me to Bourbon Street?" Black asked.

"Just in time for Mardi Gras," Blunt said. "Just stay focused."

"Roger that," Black said.

Blunt dismissed the team and waited until Alex was at the door before asking her to come back in for a short word.

"What is it?" Alex asked as she eased into the seat next to Blunt.

He hunched over and spoke softly. "Have you made any headway into your investigation of Richard Joseph, the pro-tem of the Senate from Virginia?"

"I'm still putting together a profile of him, but I'm finding it difficult to dig up much stuff. He must have one hell of a cleaner swabbing the deck of his digital misdeeds."

"He does, but keep working on it," Blunt said. "I have a feeling he might be more important than we know."

CHAPTER 5

HAWK STRAIGHTENED HIS designer sunglasses and adjusted his tie once he settled into his seat in the limousine. His stylish suit was one Black had recommended. Looking the part of a multi-millionaire real estate mogul who split his time between New York and Los Angeles required a little extra attention to detail. He glanced at Alex, who wore a stunning red dress with a fur coat, accented with a diamond necklace and dangling earrings.

He gave the driver directions and leaned back.

"You look great," Alex said as she patted his knee.

Hawk sighed. "If truth be told, I'd rather be racing around the desert, shooting terrorists. This isn't the life for me."

She smiled. "Why am I not surprised?"

"Are you seriously into this?"

"I'd probably get tired of this after a while, but I don't mind living a posh lifestyle, even if it's only for a few hours."

Hawk leaned forward. "You know what I wouldn't mind doing? Burning this suit after this is all over with."

"It's not a straightjacket," she said. "Besides, I think you look rather dapper."

"I look more dapper when I'm holding my gun."

Alex shrugged. "If you say so. I just don't want to hear any more bellyaching about what you have to wear or that you have to ride in a limo."

Hawk grunted. "I'd rather be driving."

"It's New York City, hun. I think we'd both rather not be here at all."

He flashed a smile and held Alex's hand. She understood him like nobody else and was on the same page as him, even if she did enjoy dressing up and pretending to be filthy rich.

A half hour later, they arrived at the offices for A Hand Up. They were located in a towering office building in Manhattan. Hawk and Alex took the elevator up to the fortieth floor and entered the lobby. A woman with dark hair tightly cropped against the side of her face and wearing a headset greeted them.

"May I help you?" she asked.

"Yes," Alex said. "We're here to meet Mr. Reese."

"Do you have an appointment?"

"I called yesterday about making a sizable contribution to your organization. We're the Davenports."

"Ah, yes, Alistair and Claudia," the receptionist said. "Just one moment. Let me get Mr. Reese."

Hawk and Alex sat on the couch and waited for a moment until the head of the New York office emerged with a smile on his face. He strode over to them and shook their hands.

"Milton Reese," he said. "It's so nice to meet both of you."

Hawk nodded. "Likewise, Mr. Reese."

"Please, just call me Milton. Now back this way."

He led them to his office, which was situated in the corner and overlooked a portion of New York's sprawling concrete jungle.

"Beautiful view, isn't it?" Reese asked.

Hawk nodded. "It's majestic. How on Earth do you ever get anything done?"

Reese shrugged. "That's the million-dollar question. But the truth is I have Becca, who welcomed you up front. If it wasn't for her, I don't know what I'd do."

"I'm sure you'd figure out a way to manage," Alex said.

Reese smiled and gestured toward the small couch positioned across the room next to a pair of chairs. "Do you mind if we sit over her and talk? I prefer to discuss these matters as if we were in my own home. But my home doesn't have a view even close to being this spectacular."

Hawk and Alex complied as they sat cozily on the small sofa with Reese taking a chair across from them.

"Now I must confess that until you called yesterday, I'd never heard of either of you," Reese began. "But I am impressed with what I learned about you since then."

"We do like to keep a low profile," Hawk said. "I'm sure you understand."

"Of course," Reese said. "The moment anyone learns that you have money, you're being hounded by everyone for your last nickel. I'm sure that's tiresome."

"More than you know," Alex said as she turned up her nose and rolled her eyes. "I'd rather just write them a check for a hundred thousand if they promise never to return."

Reese's eyes widened. "Well, I certainly wouldn't want to come across like that. However, I am curious about why you're so interested in donating to our organization."

Alex nodded and leaned forward in her seat. "Alistair and I have been disturbed by the growing lack of income equality in our country. And while some may find it ironic since we're supposedly part of the problem, we'd actually like to be part of the solution."

"That's very noble of you, Mrs. Davenport," Reese said.

"Please, call me Claudia. I'm not an old spinster just yet."

"Okay then, Claudia. I'm honored that you would consider A Hand Up for a charitable contribution. Is there anything else that you might want to know about our organization first?"

Hawk nodded. "As a matter of fact, there is. We happened to stumble across A Hand Up while searching for non-profits that work to eliminate income inequality by breaking cycles of poverty. And while you tout your successful work on your website, we had a difficult time finding much about what you do in the general media. If you're having so much success, why aren't there more stories out there about what you're doing? I mean, I work in real estate, and aside from the mantra of *location, location, location,* every good realtor knows he's only as good as his marketing, both of his skills and his offerings."

Reese drew a deep breath before answering. "The truth is we don't want to manage hundreds of small donations because everyone in the non-profit world knows that chasing down twenties and fifties isn't going to help you ultimately accomplish your goals. And that's what you get when you spend money to tell everyone how great you are. We generally seek out donations privately from foundations and philanthropic-minded individuals like you."

"That's understandable," Alex said. "If you're going to be successful, you have to understand your revenue stream and how to make that best work for you."

"Exactly," Reese said. "And the fact that you understand that makes me all the more excited to accept your gift, that is if you are still serious about considering A Hand Up."

"Of course we are," Hawk said.

"Well, in that case, I don't want to pressure you or anything of that nature, but we do have an amazing opportunity if you are considering making your donation within the next week," Reese said.

"What kind of opportunity?" Alex asked.

"We have a very generous donor who's agreed to not only match any gift within the next week but triple it with a corresponding donation. In other words, your one hundred thousand dollar gift could become a four hundred thousand dollar gift. And that money would go to aiding hundreds of people who sstruggle to escape poverty's grip on their lives."

"Only a hundred thousand?" Hawk asked. "Is that all you were expecting out of us?"

"Well, I've learned not to make any assumptions," Reese said.

"Oh, stop it," Alex said, playfully hitting Hawk. "You're just itching to tell him how much we've considered giving this great organization, aren't you?"

Hawk shrugged and smiled. "You know me so well, dear. But you know we're not quite ready to make this donation today. However, I would like to hear the terms of that triple gift match once more. How long do we have?"

"One week from today," Reese said. "Again, I don't want to pressure you, but it would be an incredible opportunity for us to expand so many of the programs we have here in the city."

Hawk stood and offered his hand to Alex, who joined him. "Thank you for your time, Mr. Reese. I appreciate you answering my questions. You have a lovely charity here, and we're excited about making a contribution that will help further your efforts. I'll be in touch—and it will be within a week, that much I can promise you."

Reese ushered his two potential donors to the door and thanked them profusely. Hawk and Alex hustled down the steps to the limo that was waiting for them just outside and didn't say a word until they got inside.

"We need to call Blunt," Hawk said.

Alex nodded in agreement. "Something big is going down next week."

"And we need to be ready to stop it," Hawk said.

CHAPTER 6

New Orleans, Louisiana

BLACK AWOKE EARLY and hustled out of his hotel toward Café Du Monde in the French Market. The streets were relatively empty at seven o'clock in the morning as most tourists were still recovering from a night of revelry. Outside the bars, workers swept the sidewalks as they cleaned in preparation for another wave of customers eager to drink the day away. Dodging piles of trash bags and ambitious joggers out for a run, Black rounded the corner and was blasted by the wafting smell of his favorite beignets. He didn't come to New Orleans for the food, but it was a savory perk.

Black placed his order and waited patiently at one of the tables in the open-air section of the restaurant. Pigeons strutted around in search of stray crumbs or half-eaten pastries that had tumbled to the ground. While most people stared at their phones while eating,

Black took the time to survey the clientele. It wasn't necessary, but it helped him keep his mind sharp. He saw a pair of undercover detectives as well as one pimp and two drug dealers mixed in with a sea of business professionals, both young and old. Everyone of them piqued Black's interest to some degree as he wondered about their stories. Why was the elderly gentleman in a three-piece suit eating with a sharply dressed woman who was at least forty years his junior? Or what was the story of the anorexic-looking girl with tattoos covering her arms and legs, eating alone and reading a Tolstoy novel? He enjoyed visiting Du Monde as much for the vast array of customers as he did for the food. But he wasn't in New Orleans for either. He was here to capture Fortner.

Black finished his food and headed toward Bourbon Street and all the potential recent sales of homes that fit the timeframe for when Fortner appeared to start preparing an exit strategy. In the past eighteen months, there were a dozen homes sold along Bourbon Street, most of them condo-style residences located above various establishments. Black considered asking around, but he figured Fortner would never be careless and get chummy with his neighbors. If anything, he would keep a low profile— or maybe even a non-existent one. His approach would be a smart one: The fewer people who knew about him, the better. Questioning others living in the area would likely be a waste of time.

Where are you, General?

Black meandered up and down Bourbon Street for the better part of an hour before he sat down on a bench and tried to consider all the possibilities. Fortner wouldn't want to live above a bar, at least he wouldn't given the reason for purchasing his home in such a location. He'd want to be near a watering hole, but he wouldn't frequent an establishment so often that everyone knew his name and his story.

Black wracked his brain, trying to think about which place made the most sense. Then he remembered something he'd seen at Fortner's farm in Chile: a sign for barbecue. "Maurice's Fine BBQ" was plastered across the front of a tin that was tacked to the outside of Fortner's barn. And while there wasn't a Maurice's BBQ in New Orleans, there were well-known barbecue joints located along the famed street. But Black hadn't noticed any of the addresses on his list located near such an eatery. He needed to double check.

He trekked up and down Bourbon again, striking off each address that didn't fit the criteria. When he was finished, Black was left with nothing. Frustrated by the lack of any apparent match, he followed the smell emanating from a billowing hickory wood fire a couple of blocks away. Mickey Ray's BBQ was the source.

Black surveyed the outside of the building, which had two stories located above with a decorative wrought-iron fence demarcating the edge of the balcony. He admired the exquisite handiwork, a signature of the French Quarter architecture.

"She's a beauty, ain't she?" asked a man, nudging Black with an elbow.

Black turned to look at the stranger, who had his attention turned toward the upper floors of the restaurant.

"If I lived there, I swear I'd be a hundred pounds overweight within a year," Black said.

The man rubbed his rotund belly and shook his head. "Or you could live across the street from this place like me and add twenty pounds a year for a decade."

Black stopped gawking at the structure and turned his gaze toward the man. "You've lived on Bourbon Street for a decade?"

"It's quite a feat," he said. "If you don't overdose or get shot, you've got to be doing something right. That's why I figure overeatin' is the least of my worries."

Black chuckled. "I hope they don't let you write the marketing material for the French Quarter tourism department."

"This place would probably be a ghost town if visitors knew only half of what actually goes on here."

"Yet here you are."

The man nodded. "And here's where I'll die, maybe even tonight. You just never know."

"Mitch Harrison," Black said as he offered his hand. "One of those tourists who doesn't want to know just everything yet."

"Chuck Cormier," the man said, taking Black's hand. "It's a pleasure to meet you, especially someone who appreciates New Orleans for what it truly is: A national treasure."

"It's hard not to have a good time in this city."

"I came here one weekend fifteen years ago and never left."

Black nodded. "Say, Chuck, how long did you say you've been living across the street from this restaurant?"

"For the last decade. I've seen some crazy changes around here, but that place just keeps chugging along, serving the finest barbecue in the state."

"So, is this the kind of place where you get to know all your neighbors?"

Chuck shrugged. "Depends on what they're here for. If they're here for a good time, yes. If they're here to hide, nope."

"People come here to hide?"

"Either to hide or to party. New Orleans is a great place to disappear into. You make lots of friends every night, but they don't have to know your name, though most of them wouldn't remember it in the morning anyway."

"That's a fair point. So, what about your neighbors here? Do you know all of them?"

"Most of them," Chuck said. "The guy who lives on the top floor over this restaurant ain't the friendliest fella on the planet."

"And he's been there a while?"

"Not exactly. His stepfather owned it and I guess gave it to him after he died somewhat unexpectedly about a year ago. I thought the house would go on the market, but it never did. Then the next thing you know, this hard-ass type is marching around the balcony up there like he's getting ready to pick someone off with a sniper rifle. He's always got a drink in his hand but never a smile on his face."

"Have you seen him around here the past few days?" Black asked.

Chuck eyed Black cautiously, looking him up and down. "Are you some kinda cop?"

"Just a friend looking for a friend," Black said.

"You must not be that close if he's trying to hide from you."

"You're the one who said people come here to hide. I've been trying to track him down for a while. The rest of his family has been worried sick about him. I'm just trying to get a handle on the situation."

"Well, I haven't seen him in the past week, but that doesn't mean he's not here. Just be careful. He always looks unstable. I mean, I wouldn't be surprised to wake up one morning and see him splattered all over Bourbon Street if you know what I mean."

"You have vivid imagery there, Chuck," Black said, patting the man on the back. "I'd love to buy you a drink sometime this week."

"How 'bout a two-meat, two-side platter to go along with that drink?"

"I like how you think. I'll find you later."

With that, Black headed into the bar kitty corner from Fortner's place and settled into a chair on the balcony. It was the perfect spot to casually keep an eye on everything the traitor was up to, if he was even in town.

* * *

JUST AFTER 4:00 A.M., Black sauntered down the steps and onto Bourbon Street again. There were still a handful of Mardi Gras partygoers milling around, shuffling from one pub to the next, but there hadn't been the slightest hint that Fortner was at home. Once Black was satisfied that no one was paying him any attention or too drunk to see straight, he eased into the alleyway and found the door leading upstairs to the home on the third floor. He picked the lock and crept inside.

Black searched through Fortner's desk in search of any clue that would reveal what his plans were. But after a thorough search, Black found nothing. Out of frustration, he slammed the drawer shut. Then he paused.

Well, look what we have here.

Black noted the hollow sound and immediately re-opened the drawer. He tapped on it to confirm his suspicion of a false bottom. Using his pocket knife, he pried open the lid to reveal the secret compartment that contained a folder and an address book. Black set them on the desk and started reading.

Detailed in the document was the master plan for how Obsidian would seek to boost its financial portfolio by controlling world markets. Black's eyes were glued to the pages, fascinated by the scope of the ambitious endeavor. While the endgame wasn't anything novel, Black had only seen groups attempt to use war as a way to profit from an uptick in sales for a certain commodity, never the other way around. Obsidian aimed to use terrorist threats and acts of war as a way to create a volatile market that one could profit from significantly.

Alex will love digging through this.

Black moved on to the address book, which contained mostly initials and post office boxes from countries all over the world. The two items combined told a starkly different story than the one Fortner tried to tell in Chile. He wasn't a helpless victim or some cog in the wheel. No, he was high up on the chain of command within Obsidian, though Black doubted at the highest level. He concluded that Fortner lacked the sophistication and knowledge of the economic sector's inner workings to hatch such a scheme.

After capturing every page on the camera on his phone, Black was more eager than ever to capture Fortner. And knew just the way to do it.

CHAPTER 7

Washington, D.C.

LATER THE NEXT DAY, the Phoenix Foundation team convened to discuss the results of the simultaneous operations. Alex was the first to the conference room, interested to share what she'd learned regarding her deep dive on A Hand Up's financials for the past few years. She found their spikes in contributions interesting, if not suspicious. However, the fact that it was all tidy and apparently above board made her wonder if she was just seeing what she wanted to or if A Hand Up had someone in the IRS shielding them from an audit.

Hawk brought her a cup of coffee and sat next to her as they waited for the rest of the team to enter the room. Black and Blunt followed in short order, and they began rehashing the events of the past twenty-four hours.

"Everything is beginning to come into focus,"

Alex said. "Obsidian is attempting to do exactly what we thought they were going to do—and now we know how they plan to do it."

Hawk leaned back in his chair and interlocked his fingers behind his head. "The real question now is if we're able to stop it and eliminate these people."

"Exactly," Blunt said, pointing at Hawk. "This whole thing is going to be dicey since we're talking about making prominent people disappear."

"Disappear is a euphemism, right?" Black asked. "These bastards need to be put down. They're the sickest kind of people, profiting off death and destruction. And there needs to be a reckoning."

"Agreed," Blunt said. "But we're going to have to do this our way. The circle of people who know about this needs to be small. Plausible deniability must be something we consider when it comes to who we tell and who we don't. And President Young is one of those people who can't find out what we're up to."

"I think we need to let him know about Fortner," Hawk said. "After all, Young was the one who picked Fortner to head up things at the Pentagon."

Blunt grunted as he chewed on his cigar. "We can tell Young after the fact. This intel needs to be kept in this room unless it's absolutely necessary to bring others in."

"Sounds like the best way to proceed to me," Black said.

"Is there anything else you feel we need to know before calling it a day?" Blunt asked.

Black nodded and connected his phone to the monitor on the far wall. "Before we split, I wanted to see if anyone recognized any of these addresses here in Washington?"

He scrolled through the images he took from Fortner's address book with a Washington, D.C. zip code. The team collectively shook their heads as Black flipped from one image to the next.

"Wait a minute," Blunt said. "Go back one."

Black swiped to the image Blunt requested. "See something there, boss man?"

"The one at the top," Blunt said, pointing at the screen. "I recognize that street and number."

"Is this some spy we should know about?" Hawk asked.

"Not exactly," Blunt said. "That belongs to one Catherine Tiller, better known as Kitty Tiller."

"Is that an exotic dancer stage name?" Alex asked.

Blunt cracked a wry smile. "She is known as a man-eater, ruining the livelihoods of several politicians in this city, some even before their careers got off the ground."

"And how is she significant in all this?" Hawk asked. "She doesn't seem to fit the profile of the types of people we're seeing affiliated with Obsidian."

"She's certainly not an operative, if that's what you mean," Blunt said. "However, I happen to know Fortner was in a relationship with her, something he kept very secretive."

"But you knew," Alex said.

Blunt winked. "I know everything about everyone in this town. Good luck trying to keep a secret from me."

"Maybe this address book is worthless then," Black said.

"I wouldn't jump to that conclusion just yet," Blunt warned with the wag of his finger. "It could be a mix of people associated with Obsidian as well as people who might be willing to hide him out for a few days when he's on the run."

"He's slippery," Black said. "If he's this well connected around the world, we're going to have a hard time pinning him down."

Blunt shrugged. "Maybe, maybe not. If there's anyone he'll tell what he's up to, it's Kitty Tiller."

"Think he's there now?" Hawk asked.

"There's only way to find out," Blunt said. "I'm sending you and Black on a stakeout of her apartment tonight. So go home and get some rest and then plan on spending the night together drinking coffee and keeping each other awake with your most imaginative stories while you keep an eye on her place."

"Sounds like barrels of fun," Hawk said.

Alex laughed. "So sorry I have to miss out on that, boys. I'll think about you while I'm in my bed and snug asleep."

"Not so fast, Alex," Blunt said. "I want you to analyze all this information that Black brought back from New Orleans. See if you can find market correlations with world events on those days. We need to find out exactly how Obsidian is manipulating the market."

Alex saluted Blunt. "Aye, aye, Cap'n."

"This is not how I envisioned spending my evening," Hawk said.

"Are you complaining, Hawk?" Blunt asked.

Hawk shook his head.

"Good, because if you are, I've got an undercover assignment I can give you that requires you to wear high heels and makeup," Blunt said with a grin.

"No, sir, I'm good. Black and I will have a fabulous time tonight."

Blunt stood and clapped. "Well, let's get to it. We've got a world to save, people."

* * *

ALEX CREATED A SPREADSHEET with dates that corresponded with spikes in A Hand Up's financial fortunes. One column listed all the large donations and the dates they were made. Another column was reserved for major world events, such as terrorist attacks and suicide bombers. It didn't take her long to realize that each spike was about a month to the day after each incident, confirming what Black suspected from reading Obsidian's white paper. She wondered if it was even possible to reverse the organization's fortunes. And even if it were, what would the collateral damage be? More people losing their retirement savings in the stock market? Creating worldwide financial instability? The better option seemed like a systematic elimination of the people behind this power grab.

Alex cobbled together some reports and printed them out. She was tired and ready to go home when she received a notification that the printer required more paper.

Just when I thought I'd get home at a decent hour . . .

She trudged off to the supply room and found an open ream of paper. After grabbing a handful, she noticed a body camera on the shelf. She usually processed all the video captured from Hawk's mission but hadn't been given any footage from his trip to Dubai. Curious as to how the operation looked when she lost contact with him, she grabbed it to look at while the spreadsheets finished printing.

Alex removed the chip that recorded all the

action and slid it into the slot in her computer. A few seconds later, she was skimming through Hawk's mission. First the spill on Littleton's suit followed by the incident in the bathroom. It all appeared just like it was reported. However, she furrowed her brow when she heard Hawk talking about how the connection was bad. Her voice sounded crystal clear in the footage, which was taken straight from Hawk's coms. Then Hawk's response seemed to be cutting in and out, but the ambient background noise wasn't.

What the—?

She skimmed ahead in the video and found Hawk communicating with Blunt and talking about cutting Alex out of the loop. Moving ahead, she saw Hawk's perspective as he sat in another restaurant and watched her half brother Shane Samuels dine with Andrei Orlovsky.

Alex fumed over the fact that not only had Hawk hid this extra part of his mission from her but that he conspired with Blunt to keep her in the dark. While she wasn't sure how she felt about Samuels, she hated being deceived, especially by the two people she trusted the most.

She made a screenshot of Samuels and Orlovsky eating together and printed it out.

"We're going to have a little word about this," she said as she snatched the picture off the printer.

CHAPTER 8

HAWK WARMED HIS HANDS with his cup of coffee as he eyed the entrance to Kitty Tiller's apartment. He glanced over at Black, who was seated behind the steering wheel and wore a faint smile.

"What are you so happy about?" Hawk asked. "We're stuck in this car for who knows how long, staring at a building. Don't you have other things you'd rather be doing?"

Black's grin grew wider as he shook his head. "You're an old married fogey, Hawk, with a beautiful bride waiting at home. Catching the bad guys is what I'm hitched to for now and probably the foreseeable future."

"I doubt Alex is up waiting for me. She's probably still at the office, poring over all those documents you collected in New Orleans."

"Maybe you're losing your fire for this job," Black said. "We're *this* close to catching Fortner and starting to peel back the layers on Obsidian."

"I've still got plenty of passion when it comes to serving my country, but watching the apartment of some Washington madam isn't exactly how I'd prefer to do it."

Black shrugged. "It's not all about bullets and bravery. Sometime patience and persistence are just as important, if not more so."

"Are you writing fortune cookies in your spare time?" Hawk asked.

"You're digging my succinct nuggets of wisdom, aren't you? I'll be sure to write that one down later to pass it along to all the children I'm never going to have."

"You just seem a little too amped up for this assignment, that's all."

"Well, I do have some history with Kitty Tiller," Black said.

"History? Did you—"

"Oh, no. Nothing like that. But I was working an assignment once where she was involved with this senator who I was shadowing. I've met her several times. She's a pleasant woman, even if she is a preying opportunist. I find her ilk disgusting. However, men who fall into her clutches are stupid, especially with the reputation she now has. And the fact that Fortner ever got involved with her in the first place makes me question his wisdom. He certainly knows better."

"Maybe he knew exactly what he was doing and was using her."

"Let's not give Fortner that much credit just yet. I don't think he sought out any of this business with Obsidian. It's far more likely that he was just a vulnerable man in a key role."

"You might be right, but he's been more than competent when it comes to avoiding capture," Hawk said. "He's been two or three steps ahead of us."

"He was ripping pages right out of the Obsidian playbook for coercing cooperation. Now that his tactic has been exposed, we can plan ahead too. And I don't think he ever thought we'd find his hideout in New Orleans. That might've never even been a place we considered to look had we not had such good fortune."

Hawk laughed. "I wouldn't exactly call getting pounded into pulp good luck."

"But meeting Liling was definitely was since she pointed us toward New Orleans."

"And here we are, sitting outside Kitty Tiller's apartment, just waiting for him to show up," Hawk said before he sighed.

"It makes sense that he'd come here, especially if he was working with her before. She might be gathering some kind of intel to help him or simply needing a place to lay low in Washington while he manipulates someone else to do some of Obsidian's bidding."

Hawk leaned forward in his seat, squinting as he watched the dimly lit street. "Look over there. Is that him?"

Black peered through his binoculars. "That's him all right. What is he doing?"

"Does he have a key?" Hawk asked.

"It looks like he's waiting for someone to open the door."

"Let's get him."

As Hawk went to open the door, he jumped back as a shadowy figure slapped a piece of paper against the window.

"Alex?" Hawk said as he furrowed his brow. "What are you doing here?"

"Look at this," she said. "I want to know what *you* were doing *there*."

"Fortner just showed up. Let's talk about this later."

"We've been made," Black said. "He's running."

Alex stepped away from the door and made room for Hawk to open it. He and Black tore down the street after Fortner.

"Which way did he go?" Hawk asked.

"He cut down that alley right there," Black said.

"I'll go around the backside and wait for you to flush him out."

"Sounds like a plan."

Hawk sprinted around the back of the building before he found a spot behind a dumpster to ambush Fortner. Staying completely still, Hawk tilted his head to one side and listened for the sound of footsteps. Other than a dog barking a block away or a police siren wailing down the street, the area was relatively quiet. And there weren't any footfalls clattering against the concrete.

"You found him yet?" Hawk whispered in his coms.

"No," Black said. "He must've gone in a different direction. I don't see any sign of him."

"Should I abandon my post and search the streets?" Hawk asked.

"That's probably our best option at this point. I'll keep going this way, but if he's in front of me, he's doing a good job of staying out of sight."

"Well, I haven't heard anything that remotely sounds like someone running."

"Damn it," Black said. "Where could he have gone so quickly? It's like he vanished."

Hawk's ears perked up at the sound of feet scuffling against the asphalt. "Wait. I think I hear something. Keep moving this way."

Hawk crouched low as he kept his gaze focused on the open area just beyond where he was positioned. He turned off the safety on his gun and wrapped both hands around it.

Come to daddy.

The sound stopped. Hawk put his face against the ground and eyed the pair of shoes visible beneath the wheels of the dumpster. Designer Italian leather dress shoes.

The man spun on his heels and headed in the opposite direction.

"Get ready," Hawk whispered over the coms. "He's headed back toward you."

Hawk crept into the alleyway and drew his weapon, ready to take out Fortner if fired upon.

"Put those hands up where I can see them," Hawk said.

The man turned around slowly and raised one hand in the air, while the other was holding a toy poodle.

"What is the meaning of this?" the man asked. "I'm just out for an evening stroll with Mr. Rockerfeller."

Hawk holstered his weapon. "I apologize, sir. Wrong place, wrong time. I thought you were someone else."

Before Hawk could say anything else, a car roared out of the alley behind him.

"False alarm," Hawk said. "But I think he just drove out of here and is on the street. I'm in pursuit."

Hawk pumped his arms as he increased his stride

until he reached full speed. His lungs strained to process the cold air while his legs burned from sudden burst toward the street.

By the time he reached the sidewalk to get a clear view, the car's tires were screeching as it rounded the corner. He looked behind him to see Black slowing to a stop next to Alex, who had apparently been taking in the whole scene.

"If you were at your computer, we might be able to track where he was going," Hawk said.

"If you didn't keep secrets from me, I never would've come down here in the first place," she fired back. "How can I even trust you anymore?"

"Alex, it's not like that," Hawk said.

She wasn't hearing any of it, turning around and storming back toward their car.

Black continued to move toward Hawk. "Don't worry about it, man. We'll get Fortner another time."

"But that was our golden opportunity to capture him. We may not get another chance like that."

Black shrugged. "We will. Now go sort things out with Alex. We need this team on the same page if we're going to take down Obsidian."

Hawk sighed and trudged toward the car. But Alex was already gone.

CHAPTER 9

HAWK GROANED WHEN his alarm went off the next morning. After training himself to get up at daybreak while in the military, Hawk rarely slept late enough for his alarm to sound. But between sleeping on the couch and rehashing his conversation with Alex in his head, he was up for hours before finally crashing.

He rolled off the edge, hitting the floor with a thud. Usually such a noise would have Alex running into the room, sometimes with her gun drawn. But not this morning. Alex had already left for the day.

Hawk scrambled to get dressed and cooked breakfast before heading to the office. And it wasn't something he was looking forward to. His only hope was that Alex had cooled off some and would be a little more understanding.

When Hawk strode through the front doors at the Phoenix Foundation, he received some looks that signaled he knew Alex had already charged inside in all her fury. A couple of administrative assistants glanced at him then looked away when he made eye contact, hiding behind their project reports and manila folders. There was nothing he could do but brace for Hurricane Alex, not that he really blamed her for her anger.

Hawk crept past her workstation, crouching low and moving swiftly until he reached Blunt's office. He softly knocked on the door and eased inside.

Blunt grunted as Hawk slipped into one of the chairs across from his boss's desk.

"Please keep it down," Hawk said in a hushed tone. "If she hears you talking, she's going to storm in here."

Blunt took a long pull on his coffee before setting it down on the table and emitting a satisfied sigh. "I knew this was coming, but I had no idea it'd be this rough. Alex is usually a pretty understanding person."

"Except when it comes to issues of honesty. When she's been lied to or feels like someone tried to pull one over on her, she brings some fire."

"Have you had a chance to talk with her yet?" Blunt asked.

Hawk shook his head slowly. "I slept on the couch last night because I know a conversation wouldn't go anywhere. To be honest, I didn't even attempt to discuss it last night after we got back from our stakeout of Kitty Tiller's place."

"Black gave me the full report on how that went," Blunt said as he winced. "How did Fortner escape?"

"Hell if I know. For a minute there, I thought we had him pinned down. And then *poof!* It was like he disappeared into thin air. I know we're not dealing with some rookie operative, but I certainly didn't expect him to behave like a seasoned agent."

"You can't underestimate Fortner," Blunt said. "He's got a way about him that suggests he's just bumbling along. But I think that's his way of creating lower expectations all around for himself. Then when he exceeds those expectations, you think he's a damn magician."

"Well, he had to have some magic working last night to elude us. We were right on top of him before he inexplicably escaped."

"Hopefully we'll get another chance soon," Blunt said. "But in the meantime—"

"In the meantime, you better start looping me in on everything," Alex said as she burst into the room.

Blunt held up his hands, gesturing for her to calm down. "Alex, we're all on the same side here."

"Then why does it feel like I'm being ostracized?" she said, stamping her foot. "I work hard for this team, and I'm just as much of a part of it as anyone else. Keeping me in the dark isn't the way we need to operate."

Blunt clipped off the end of a cigar and then stuffed the stogie into his mouth. "Alex, this is exactly why I didn't want to tell you what Hawk was doing."

"What?" Alex said.

"*This*, this reaction," Blunt said, extending his hand toward her and circling her in the air. "When you act like this, it makes everyone more reticent to trust you. Stomping around the office, disrupting a stakeout—we feared that you'd be a little fiery if you learned that your brother was being investigated."

"First of all, he's my half brother," Alex said, pointing her index finger at Blunt. "And secondly, I'm not mad because you suspected him and asked Hawk to look into what he was doing. I'm mad because you intentionally hid it from me. You conspired with my *husband* to keep a portion of his mission away from me. I find that infuriating."

Blunt shifted in his seat. "Well, perhaps I made a mistake, but I—"

"No, you definitely made a mistake," Alex said. "What makes this team work so well is the fact that we have each other's backs and don't keep secrets from each other."

"Alex, we're in the espionage business," Blunt

said. "You should know by now that secrecy is a part of what we do."

"But from each other? No, that's not how this works. At least, that's not how it's supposed to work. We can't have any doubt that we're all on the same page and have the same goals for each mission—and even if it's family."

Blunt's eyebrows shot upward. "Are you sure about that?"

Alex nodded. "I signed up to protect the security interests of this country and the people who serve it, no exceptions. Full stop."

"In that case, let me offer you a sincere apology," Blunt said. "I never should have made a decision based out of fear of how you'd react. Can you trust me again?"

She sighed and crossed her arms. "I hope so."

"And look, I'm not a marriage counselor, but it might be a good idea if you and Hawk—"

"Save it," Hawk and Alex said in unison. They both glanced at each other and broke into a grin.

"You're still probably sleeping on the couch tonight," she said.

Before Hawk could respond, an alarm on Alex's phone started buzzing. She picked it up and pumped her fist triumphantly.

"What is it?" Hawk asked.

"This is exactly why you shouldn't have kept me out of the loop and should know you can trust me with anything," Alex said, showing her cell screen to Hawk and Blunt.

"What's all that gibberish mean?" Blunt asked.

"That *gibberish* is code I wrote to search for any aliases that my brother—"

"Half brother," Blunt said.

Alex smiled. "Yes, I wrote a code to search for any aliases my half-brother uses so we could track him down."

"Where is he?" Hawk asked.

"Let's go have a look," Alex said before dashing out of the room and toward her computer terminal.

Blunt and Hawk followed closely behind her.

"That went better than I'd hoped," Blunt said in a whisper to Hawk.

"I don't want to hear your gloating right now," Hawk said. "I'm obviously still in the dog house, and who knows when I'll get out of it."

Hawk stood back and watched as Alex hammered away on the keyboard to call up the information related to her alert. He loved working with her, especially when they had good chemistry. But given all that had just transpired, he hoped that Blunt's idea to keep Alex in the dark about the shadow mission of Samuels didn't cause everything to unravel.

All Hawk could do was trust that their relationship was bigger than a spy spat.

"Where is he?" asked Blunt, who started drumming his fingers on her desk.

"Well, would you look at that?" Alex said, tapping her monitor. "Good ole Max Ellington is back from the dead. He bought a burner phone in New York City that's easily tracked. And guess who he called first?"

"The Russian embassy?" Blunt asked.

"That's a lazy guess," Alex said. "He called A Hand Up and our good friend, Mr. Reece."

"If we weren't sure before, there's no doubt that charity is shady," Hawk said.

"But that's not all," Alex said.

Blunt squinted as he stooped over and stared at the screen. "There's more?"

"I just got a printout of their conversation," Alex said.

Blunt went slack-jawed. "How'd you—"

"I've still got some good friends at the NSA," Alex said with a wry grin. "According to this message, they're meeting this morning."

Blunt snapped his fingers. "In that case, I want the two of you on a train to New York by noon. See if you can press Reece for information about one Max Ellington."

"What about Black?" Hawk asked. "We might

need him for support if things get messy."

Blunt shook his head. "I'm confident you two can handle Reece. Besides, I've got another assignment for Black."

Hawk waited until Blunt left the room before saying anything. "Can you run home with me and get everything you need?"

Alex nodded. "Yes, but you're not off the hook just yet."

Hawk's phone buzzed, and he ignored it. When Alex wasn't looking, he snuck a peek at the screen and then quickly shoved the device back into his pocket.

CHAPTER 10

BLACK DESCENDED THE STEPS as he entered Off the Record, a cocktail bar in the basement of the Hay-Adams Hotel and frequented by Washington's elite. He recognized a pair of senators from opposing parties huddled at a table in the back while sharing a drink. According to his watch, it was only 4:00 p.m., but the place was nearly full.

A man approached Black and slapped him on the back before draping an arm over his shoulder. Black scowled as he looked down at the man.

"I've been watching you," the man said. "You've been here less than a minute and still don't have a drink in your hand. It's obvious that you're not from around here."

"What makes you say that?" Black asked.

"If you were, you'd already be halfway through your first drink. It's the only way to keep your sanity while working in Washington."

"If you need to drink to stay sane, perhaps you should consider a change in profession."

The man scrunched up his nose and shook his head slowly. "I've been in this town too damn long to switch now, and I sure as hell won't be able to find any other work after being a lobbyist. We're right up there with lawyers and IRS accountants as the most despised people on the planet."

Black was annoyed with the man's intrusion but decided he could still be helpful. "Have you seen Kitty Tiller here today?"

The man smiled. "Oh, now I understand why you're here."

Black sighed. "Have you seen her or not?"

The man held his glass out and pointed toward the bar. "A few minutes ago, she was sitting on the other side over there."

"Who knew lobbyists could still be so helpful," Black said, patting the man on the shoulder to earn a sideways glance. Black strode across the room toward the other side of the bar in search of Kitty.

Sitting on a stool at the far end against the wall was Kitty. She leaned forward, resting her chin on her fist as her eyes danced across the face of the neighboring man whose arms swung wildly as he talked. The moment he paused, she closed her eyes and gave a polite laugh before directing her attention to the margarita in front of her.

Black found a table nearby and ordered a glass

of water. He watched Kitty and her suitor for the next half hour. Eventually, she held up her finger and asked if he would excuse her.

Black watched her disappear around the corner in search of the restrooms. He followed her to the short corridor and waited for her to emerge. After a few minutes, she re-emerged, straightening her skirt as she did.

"Is that guy boring you to death?" Black asked.

She sighed, refusing to stop. "Sorry, fella. I've already got one lame pickup artist to ditch right now. I don't have time for two."

"Miss Tiller, I'm not trying to pick you up," he said.

She stopped and looked him in the eye.

"That is unless you're talking about the kind of pickup that involves taking a ride with me to an undisclosed location for interrogation."

She cocked her head to one side and gazed at him. "Mister—"

"Agent Black," he said.

"Agent Black, I'm not sure what you want with me, but I can assure you that many other G-men before you have tried to bring trumped up charges against me and failed. I'd hate for your name to be added to a long list of losers."

"I'm not a G-man," Black said, grabbing her by

the arm. "And I'm not trying to bring you in, but I do need to discuss a few things with you regarding your relationship with General Van Fortner."

"Who?"

Black relaxed his grip. "This is not the time to play dumb, Miss Tiller."

"Say his name again. Maybe it will jog my memory."

Black narrowed his eyes. "Van Fortner. General Van Fortner."

"Ah, yes, I think I do remember him. But I'm afraid I can't help you. I haven't seen him in a while, several months if I recall correctly."

Black decided to call her bluff. "Then how come I have surveillance footage of him entering your home as recently as this week?"

"I thought you said you weren't a G-man."

"I'm not, which means I have far better means to obtain access to video cameras in a more expeditious manner. But thanks for confirming that Fortner was at your apartment this week. I thought you said you were well versed when it came to dealing with FBI agents."

She turned fully toward Black and brushed her hand along his bicep. "Well, aren't you a sly one."

"And impervious toward your advances," Black said with a faint smile. "However, I'm still prone to marching you out of here if you don't cooperate."

"Is that a threat?" she asked, her eyes widening.

"Do you feel threatened?"

She shook her head.

"Then I guess it isn't. Consider it more of a promise that if you aren't willing to assist me in this matter, I might have to resort to other means."

"I'll do you one better. I'll just tell Fortner about your so-called promise. You'll regret you ever decided to tangle with me."

Black stroked his chin and looked skyward. "Why would you even consider defending that monster?"

"Monster?" she asked as she drew back. "General Fortner is a national treasure. He's one of the few people who understands what this country needs at this moment and is willing to make the sacrifices necessary to see a better future realized."

"The kind of sacrifices that include kidnapping innocent young women just to get his way?"

Kitty pursed her lips and shook her head. "The general would never do such a thing. That's not his style."

"Tell that to my sister," Black said. "Some of his goons abducted her just to get to me. That's exactly his style."

"No, not the general. You're just trying to get me to go along with your scheme."

Black whipped out his phone and swiped a few times until he reached the image of his sister tied up and looking like she'd just endured a few rounds in a boxing ring against a far more physical opponent.

Kitty's mouth fell agape. "Well, I—how do I know you're not lying? That just seems absurd."

"If you've been around him as much as you claim you have, I think you know the truth," Black said. "You, perhaps more than anyone, wouldn't want to go on protecting someone like that, would you?"

Black understood his confrontation with Kitty would require a thorough knowledge of his opponent. Before she became arguably Washington's most famous madam, Black learned that she had been kidnapped as a college student by one of her father's enemies in the dark underworld of illegal sports gambling in Las Vegas. She was eventually released but not until she had spent three weeks confined to a small room with just a pillow and a blanket to comfort her each night as she slept on a concrete floor. But she never saw her father again as he was killed in a car bombing the morning before her abductors let her go.

Black didn't want to lead with that information, instead skillfully guiding the conversation to that point where he could wield the past as a way to pry a gap between her and Fortner.

Kitty shook her head. "Nice try, Mr. Black. You

have the version of that story I wanted everyone to know. Unfortunately for you, the tugging on my emotional heartstrings won't work, especially since I engineered the entire episode. My father was a very abusive man, and he got a just end."

Black paused, unsure of what to say since his grand plan had just been thrown a curveball by a master manipulator.

"Wow," she said. "You're speechless, though that shouldn't be entirely surprising since I have quite a talent for making men shut up."

Black glared at her.

Kitty moved closer and patted him on the chest. "Now, I'm gonna go ditch this loser at the bar and you're going to stay right here."

Black decided his pleasant approach had gone on long enough. If he was going to get Kitty Tiller to cooperate, he needed to employ a more forceful tactic.

"No, you're coming with me," Black said as he opened up his coat and showed her his sidearm. "I'm not against carrying you out of here kicking and screaming. And if you try to make a scene, you and I both know you're not going to get the benefit of the doubt from anyone. Most importantly, I doubt it will be good for your business."

Kitty sighed and pinched the bridge of her nose. She closed her eyes and took a deep breath.

"It's very important that I find him," Black said. "Where is he, Kitty?"

"I have no idea. Like I said, I haven't seen him in a while."

"Is that so?"

"Yes, I swear to God. It's the honest truth. I haven't seen him."

"Don't lie to me," Black said. "I saw him near your apartment last night."

"Okay, look, I haven't *seen* him, but he has his own key. He's obviously around."

"Why do you say that?"

"Because he left his phone at my apartment last night."

"Do you have it with you?"

She drew a long breath and exhaled slowly. "Yeah, it's in my purse."

"I'll leave you alone and walk right out of here if you're willing to give it to me."

"Let me get it," she said.

Black kept an eye on her around the corner as she went to her seat and dug a cell phone out of her purse, ignoring the inebriated fool next to her. She returned moments later and handed it over to Black.

"Here it is," she said. "Now, I'd appreciate it if you'd leave discreetly. People over there were already asking questions about who you were."

"What's the password?" Black asked.

She shrugged. "Try my birthday."

"And what's that date?"

"You're a resourceful guy," she said with a wink. "I'm sure you can figure it out."

Black glanced at his watch. It was almost 5:00 p.m. He dialed Alex's number to pass along the good news and see if she could give him Kitty Tiller's birthdate.

After a few rings, the call went to voicemail. He tried again, and it didn't even ring before Black was listening to Alex's message once again.

Come on, Alex. Pick up your phone.

CHAPTER 11

New York City

HAWK AND ALEX HUSTLED up to A Hand Up's offices right at 4:30 p.m., hoping to catch Milton Reese before he left for the day. They arrived just in time to see him pulling the door shut and scrambling to insert his key into the deadbolt.

"Mr. Reese," Alex called, "we were hoping we'd catch you."

Reese turned around, and his wide smile dissipated as his gaze met the couple. "Mr. and Mrs. Davenport, I'm afraid I have to get going. Are you here to make a donation?"

"That's what we came down here to speak with you about," Hawk said.

"In that case, I can probably keep the office open for a few more minutes," Reese said as he pushed the door open. "Please, do come in."

Once they were inside, he relocked the doors and

slipped the keys into his pocket. "Just in case anyone else comes along, I don't want them to think we're still available. My assistant went home early with a cold, so I'm stuck with handling everything on my own today."

"Looks like you've got it under control," Alex said.

Reese ushered them into his office and gestured for them to sit in the chairs across from him. They complied as he strode around to his desk and opened up the side drawer. He retrieved a handgun and trained it on Hawk.

"Enough with the games," Reese said. "I want to know who the hell you people are because you sure as hell aren't any Davenports that I could find."

"Oh, hey now," Hawk said, gesturing for Reese to lower his weapon. "What's that? Goodness me, Mr. Reese. What's gotten into you? Perhaps you've had a rough day or you just need a stiff drink, but we have no idea what on Earth you're talking about?"

"No idea?" Reese asked as he narrowed his eyes. "Don't patronize me, *Alistair*. I know a scam when I see one—and you two are running some sort of game. And I refuse to be taken advantage of."

"We don't want any trouble," Alex said. "We just want to help, but I'm not so sure now."

Sweat beading up on his forehead, Reese remained on his feet, bouncing his gun back and forth between Hawk and Alex.

"Please put that away," Hawk said, his hands still raised. "We just stopped by to chat. But maybe I need to find another charity to donate all this money to."

"Enough with the charades," Reese said. "You're both lying, and I can prove it."

"Prove what?" Alex asked, the tension in her voice rising. "I believe you told me that you looked into us and everything checked out. We're the ones who want to give you money."

"Sometimes you just need to take a closer look," Reese said. He opened a folder on his desk and spun the stack of documents around so they could see them. On top was a photo of Alex and Hawk both slinking down an alleyway with their weapons drawn.

Hawk waved dismissively at the picture. "Look, I don't know why anyone would feel the need to concoct such a story against us, but that image has clearly been worked over by Photoshop. I mean, I do sometimes carry a gun when I'm visiting a potential industrial property in certain sections of L.A., but we're not out hunting anyone. This is a ridiculous accusation, compounded by the fact that you feel the need to hold us at gunpoint. I can assure you that I'll be alerting non-profit watchdogs about your outlandish behavior."

"There's nothing crazy about being wise in every

circumstance," Reese said. "Now, stay put while I tie you up."

"Who told you this about us? Max Ellington?" Alex asked.

Reese paused but didn't answer before resuming his search. His momentary glance back at Alex signaled that she was right.

"If Max suggested that we're dangerous con artists, I can't tell you how rich that is," Hawk said. "I've never met a bigger thief than Mr. Ellington. He is ruthless."

"Then why didn't he wait until you already made your donation before he tried to blindside me?" Reese asked. "The fact is he knew you were never going to give me a dime, so he warned me."

"First of all, that's not true," Hawk said. "I came prepared to offer you a large check today. Just look in the right breast pocket on my blazer, and tell me what you find. Go ahead. I won't bite."

Reese fished out a check that was written to A Hand Up in the amount of two hundred fifty thousand. "There's just one problem."

"What's that?" Hawk asked.

"It's not signed."

"Of course not," Hawk said. "I always want to see how things are going before I lug around a check ready to be deposited. I wasn't born that long ago, but

I wasn't born yesterday. Now, if you let us go, I'll just sign that little check and you'll never hear from us again—ever. I promise."

Reese scratched the side of his face and crinkled up his nose as he stared off in the distance. "As tempting as that offer sounds, I value my life so much more."

"What are you going to do?" Alex asked in a breathy voice. "Call the police?"

Reese grinned slyly. "You wish. No, I'm going to handle you in a more appropriate manner for your skill set."

"Skill set?" Alex asked. "What are you going to do? Bury us on one of the properties we represent?"

Reese glared at her. "Let's cut the realtor bullshit. I know you both work for the government in some capacity as special agents. I don't even really care who. All I know is that you need to stay here while I get someone to help deal with you."

Hawk glanced at Alex and subtly shook his head.

"What's the matter, Mr. Reese?" Hawk asked. "Can't handle your own dirty work?"

"I have half a mind to shoot you right now," Reese said with a growl.

"That's way too much clean up for a man in your position. And right now, it's all hands on deck for your employer's next big move."

Reese chuckled. "You sure are tenacious, but it's not going to work with me. I'm onto your tactics and what you're trying to do here. But I'm not going to confirm or deny anything about what my *employer* is directing me to do. The only thing I've been ordered to do at the moment is collect donations and offer triple matching to every qualifying gift."

"I think we can also cut the charity bullshit, too," Hawk said. "We all know that you work for Obsidian and that the organization has a major event planned next week. And it's not going to be a simple donor drive—it's going to be a drive to fill its coffers in another method."

"That's enough," Reese said before he drew back his handgun and acted as if he was going to hit Hawk with it. The CEO relented and instead knelt behind Hawk and affixed his hands and arms to the chair, wrapping a rope around his wrists as well as his ankles and fastening them to the seat legs.

When finished with Hawk, Reese moved on to Alex and finished tying both of the once-prospective donors to their chairs.

"I hope Max was right about you," Reese said.

"Either way, you've made an enemy," Hawk said. "And you're going to regret this decision every waking hour for the short time that I allow you to keep inhaling oxygen on this planet."

"You talk a big game for someone who's going to die later today," Reese said.

"I suggest you tone it down just a little bit before I start shooting."

"I'd like to see you try," Hawk said with a sneer.

"Better quit while you're ahead," Reese said before recoiling and smacking Hawk in the head with a pistol. Hawk moaned, teetering in and out of consciousness before finally relenting and passing out.

CHAPTER 12

BLACK WAITED FOR TWO HOURS without hearing back from Hawk or Alex before he decided to call Blunt and discuss the matter. With Fortner's phone in hand, Black didn't feel like the team could afford to lose much more time if they intended to capture the renegade general. Black had tried several combinations of Kitty's birthday for the password, but none of them worked. But with only three attempts remaining before the phone locked, he decided to let someone more proficient in hacking into such devices handle the duties.

Blunt grunted when he answered the phone. "You do realize I'm in the middle of my weekly chess game, don't you?"

"Of course," Black said. "You've only been playing for a whole month now, but you haven't forgotten to mention that almost every day in the office."

"Yet here you are calling me."

"I wouldn't be doing it unless it was an emergency."

"The Russians better be raining down nukes on our heads."

"I'm sure you would've heard from someone else by now if that was the case."

"In that case, I'm gonna hang up now and get back to my game."

Black sighed. "Look, I'm sorry for interrupting you, but I need to know if you've heard from Hawk and Alex. I'm getting worried about them."

"Let me assure you that they are more than capable of handling themselves in just about every situation imaginable. Now if there isn't anything else—"

"As a matter of fact, there is." Black decided to shift tactics and pique Blunt's interest with a piece of good news.

"What is it?"

"I found Kitty Tiller."

"Big deal. I could go to Off the Record and be slurping down some fruity cocktail with her in fifteen minutes if I wanted to."

Black smiled at Blunt's bluster. "But could you pry Fortner's phone out of her hands?"

"She *gave* you his phone? Out of the goodness of her heart?"

"I may have incentivized her a bit."

"That's why you're my favorite agent."

"I think you misspoke there," Black said. "You pronounced the word *best* like the word *favorite*. Common mistake. People do it all the time with me."

"And what have you found out from getting Fortner's phone?"

"Nothing yet," Black said. "That's why I'm desperate to get in touch with Alex and Hawk. I need her to hack this thing open for me before he slips through our fingers again."

Blunt groaned. "Hell, Black, you sure know how to ruin my night out."

"You're always talking about my special set of skills," Black deadpanned.

"Let me see if I can get her to pick up, and I'll call you right back."

For the next five minutes, Black paced around the Phoenix Foundation and awaited Blunt's call. With everyone gone, Black sat down at Alex's terminal and entered his password. Then he opened up the program that tracked their cell phones. Hawk's and Alex's were listed as offline.

Black's phone buzzed. He quickly swiped it open and answered the call from Blunt.

"What'd you find out?" Black asked.

"Neither one of them are answering for me," Blunt said. "And even more troubling is the fact that

I called Mallory Kauffman to see if she could determine Alex's location from pinging her number off the cell phone towers."

"No dice?"

"Nothing. Alex's phone was last activated about a half hour ago near A Hand Up's office, which means she was there. But nothing since."

"What's your gut telling you?" Black asked.

"Get to New York and find out what's going on."

"That's what I was hoping you'd say."

"If something changes and I hear from them, I'll call you," Blunt said.

"I'll do likewise."

Black grabbed the duffle bag tucked in the back of the filing cabinet next to his desk. He had everything he needed, including enough weapons and ammo to engage in a standoff with gunmen for a couple of hours, not that he anticipated getting into a protracted gunfight. But it was always best to be prepared for anything.

Five minutes later, he roared out of the parking lot and headed for New York.

* * *

THE DRIVE WAS MONOTONOUS, though devoid of the usual traffic jam along that 250-mile stretch of interstate. Black's car hummed along, the tires bumping rhythmically as he pushed the speed limit while the Bee Gees' greatest hits album pumped through the stereo system. During his trip, he called Alex and Hawk multiple times only to get sent straight to voicemail.

Once Black reached the city, he found a parking spot along the same street as A Hand Up's offices and hunkered down for a stakeout. He ventured outside only to get a cup of coffee to combat the frigid February temperatures. By New York's standards, this city block was relatively dead, a fact that could be attributed to the weather. The most exciting activity he witnessed were shivering dog walkers hurrying along the sidewalk and the occasional police car racing by with sirens blaring.

Black took a power nap and awoke to find the street stiller than ever. But by 7:30 a.m., that started to change. And just before 8:00 a.m., Milton Reese entered the office building housing A Hand Up.

An hour later, Black straightened his tie, grabbed his briefcase, and strode into the charity's lobby. A woman with a headset on greeted him with a warm smile.

"May I help you?" she asked.

"Yes, I'm here to meet with Mr. Reese."

"And you are?"

"Arty Winchester from YCS."

"YCS?"

"Your Computing Solutions," Black said. "I had an appointment to speak with Mr. Reese regarding your organization's software."

The receptionist furrowed her brow. "I'm sorry, but I'm not seeing that on his calendar."

"Well, I spoke with him last week to confirm."

"Just have a seat," she said. "He started an important conference call a few minutes ago, but I'll try to get a message to him when I get a chance and see if he wants you to stick around or reschedule."

"Sure thing," Black said before settling into one of the chairs in the lobby.

After five minutes, he asked the receptionist where the restroom was and then sauntered off toward it. He stopped at the end of the hallway before glancing over his shoulder to see if the woman was still looking. She wasn't, so he darted to the right down another short corridor of offices.

Black jiggled the knob of a door with opaque glass, but it didn't budge. He tried another that was solid wood. Unable to open that door either, he pulled out his pick set and popped open the lock, revealing a storage area. Just as he was about to go inside, he heard footsteps coming in his direction and stopped.

A man with a furrowed brow rounded the corner and halted the moment he made eye contact with Black.

"What are you doing down here?" the man demanded.

"I'm sorry, sir," Black said. "I was searching for the restroom, and I got turned around. Is it this way?"

"Who are you?"

"Arty Winchester from YCS. I had an appointment this morning with Mr. Reese."

The man shook his head. "I'm Milton Reese, but I didn't have any appointments this morning."

Black shrugged. "I don't know. Corporate set it up. Maybe someone made a mistake somewhere."

"Or maybe you aren't who you say you are," Reese said with a growl.

"Hey, man, it's cool. Just chill out," Black said as he closed the door.

Reese looked over his shoulder before striding closer to Black and pulling out a gun.

Black threw his hands in the air. "Whoa, whoa. No need for that. If you don't want me to handle your computer problems, feel free to shop around and have someone else do it. I'm just making a sales call that came at your request."

Reese glared at Black. "Get in that room right now."

"What are you doing?" Black asked as he moved toward the door.

"Just shut up and get in there."

Black complied, keeping one of his hands raised while the other turned the knob. He backed inside to a storage room that was neatly organized with computer servers on one side and shelving units packed with office supplies on the other.

"What are you going to do to me?" Black asked, trying to act like he thought a normal civilian would in such a circumstance. "I will walk out that front door right now and never tell a soul about what just happened."

"Let me see your phone," Reese asked as he held out his hand. "Slowly, slowly."

Black reached into his pocket and fished out the device, handing it to Reese. "What are you going to do to me now?"

Reese's eyes darted back and forth. Black noticed sweat beading up on his captor's forehead as he hesitated to respond.

"Are you gonna tie me up?" Black asked.

"Shut up and let me think," Reese said, keeping his gun trained on Black.

After a long pause, Reese snatched a roll of duct tape off one of the shelves and tossed it at Black.

"What am I supposed to do with this?" Black asked.

"In a perfect world, we'd start by putting that over your mouth."

Black scowled. "Look, we both know I can't tie myself up. If you want me tied up, you're gonna have to come over here and do it yourself."

Reese stormed across the room toward his captive. Black took a few steps back, easing into a narrow aisle where rows of shelves flanked him. He figured if he could force a close-quarters combat situation, he would be able to overtake Reese.

"Stop moving," Reese commanded.

Black ignored the directive and eased back a couple more steps.

"I said *stop*!"

Once Reese entered the tight space, he staggered to his knees and fell forward with a moan. Acting quickly, Black snatched the gun from his kidnapper's hand before he hit the floor. Then Black looked up to see Hawk and Alex.

"I could've handled this myself," Black said.

"You looked like you were doing fine on your own," Alex said. "You were doing so much backing up, I almost expected to hear a beeping noise."

"That was all part of my plan," Black said. "Once I got him back here against the wall, I was going to surprise him with a throat punch and maybe add one more for good measure."

Hawk yanked Reese by his collar, lifting him to his feet. He sneered at the trio who had managed to flip the tables on him.

"You didn't really think you were going to keep us locked up for that long, did you?" Alex asked.

Black pulled Reese's hands behind his back and wrapped duct tape around them to temporarily secure him. "Is this what you were wanting me to do with this tape?"

"My secretary will be back here looking for me soon," Reese said.

"I don't think so," Alex said as she typed a message on his phone.

"What are you doing?" Reese asked.

"Making sure she leaves you alone for the next half hour since you want some pastries and coffee from the café two blocks away," she said with a wink. "And then once she leaves, I'm going to text her and tell her that you're leaving early for the day."

"What do you people want?" Reese asked. "Because I get the strange sense that you aren't looking to donate anything to A Hand Up or sell me computer software."

Hawk led Reese across the room and forced him into a chair.

"We want to know everything," Hawk said.

CHAPTER 13

Washington, D.C.

J.D. BLUNT STUFFED HIS CIGAR into his pocket as he entered Tryst, the downtown coffee shop popular among most everyone working on Capitol Hill. Even though he rarely lit up his stogies, just the presence of one would be enough to alarm some of the café's clientele. As he approached the counter to order, he scanned the area for CIA Deputy Director Randy Wood.

Just before Blunt ordered, he spotted Wood shuffling a deck of cards at a corner table. Blunt ordered his coffee and received his drink soon after. He ambled through the tables and chairs scattered across the floor and eased into a seat opposite of Wood in the back corner of the room.

"It's too early in the morning to play poker," Blunt said with a wry grin.

"Afraid you won't be able to defend your most

recent victory over me?" Wood fired back. "That win was quite some time ago, and you've been scared to play me since."

"When you win as much as I do, what's there left to prove?"

Wood chuckled and then took a sip of his drink. "It's good to see you, J.D."

"And you as well. So, to what do I owe the pleasure of this invitation?"

"I apologize for calling a meeting in a place like this, but I don't know where to go that I'd feel comfortable chatting with you about this."

Blunt furrowed his brow. "What's wrong, Randy? You're starting to worry me."

"Look, it's just that I don't know who to trust any more. Quite frankly, you're the only one outside my office that I trust. And the number of people I believe are on my side—the right side, the nation's side—I can count on one hand."

"Is this about Obsidian?"

Wood nodded. "I got a report from one of the few agents I've been able to count on over the years who found out just how far and deep their tentacles reach." He sighed before continuing. "They're everywhere, J.D. And I mean *everywhere*. They're in Congress, they're in the White House, they're in the CIA *and* FBI. It's hard to swing a stick without hitting one of them."

"That's not really news, Randy. I told you this stuff was going on a while back. What made you change your mind?"

Wood took another long pull from his mug before setting it down and responding pensively. "Look, I know you warned me about this. However, you never told me the extensive infiltration that had already occurred. Every branch of the federal government is practically under siege."

"And how do you plan on stopping them?"

"That's why I brought you here," Wood said. "I was hoping you could help come up with something creative."

"You needed to talk to me about this in person?"

Wood shifted in his seat. "Well, there's some more sensitive information I needed to discuss with you, and we had to do it in a public place."

"Just spit it out, Randy."

"My agent found out who Obsidian was recruiting next."

Blunt eyed Wood carefully as he slid a manila folder across the table. Opening the documents carefully, Blunt started to peruse the rote reports.

"Is this who I think it is?"

Wood nodded. "The first lady."

Blunt's mouth fell agape. "Madeline Young wouldn't be caught up in something like this."

"You sound surprised, J.D. And you of all people shouldn't be. You're the one who told me when I first came to Washington that I shouldn't trust anyone."

"Yet here you are, ignoring my advice by spilling the beans to me."

"The irony isn't lost on me, but I have to trust some people, though it's a really short list. And of all those names, you're the only one who can actually do something about it."

"Well, we work under the radar, but it's not like we're totally invisible. And if we get caught . . ."

Wood shrugged. "Don't you think it's worth the risk?"

"That depends on what's at stake."

"If the presidency is compromised, our nation's security is at stake. Forget what those terrorists are doing. We can't let Obsidian sink its claws into Young."

"Do want my team to eliminate the first lady?"

"Are you kidding me?" Wood asked. "She's a national treasure. Aside from the fact that she's as classy of a lady as you'll find, she flew fighters in Iraq patrolling the no-fly zone. She's not someone we want to try to remove with extreme measures."

"You want to use her then?"

"I want *you* to use her."

"Do you have any idea who's running her?"

Wood shook his head. "We have a hunch, but it's all speculation at this point. And to be honest, we came across this information by dumb luck. One of our analysts was sifting through some regular offshore deposits and traced them back to Madeline Young."

"How do you know these payments are related to Obsidian?"

"We don't for certain, but there is a deep-pockets lobbyist several of our agents believe is connected to Obsidian on some level. Henry Rutherford is a philanthropist by day and lobbyist by night for Wall Street. He maintains a low profile on Capitol Hill, but he is a puppet master, make no mistake about it. And Rutherford and the first lady have had several meetings as of late—and they haven't been about any of her children's charities or her STEM for Girls program, according to our sources. They've been closed door meetings, which is highly unusual."

"Sure there's nothing else going on?"

"No," Wood said emphatically. "Rutherford isn't about to get involved romantically with the first lady. He has multiple mistresses. But we're monitoring him very closely and think we've determined another attack will happen soon."

"That's what my team has concluded," Blunt said. "They're predicting sometime within the next week. But don't be fooled into thinking this is all about money. It's ultimately about power. And Obsidian is going to make a power grab for sure."

"Power and money are one in the same," Wood said. "But I need your team to back off a little bit."

"Back off? Right now?" Blunt's attention was briefly arrested by a text message from Hawk.

"Is everything all right?"

"I'll deal with it in a minute."

Wood nodded. "We can't charge ahead with a wide-sweeping investigation at the moment because we don't need Rutherford or the first lady to have any reason to be nervous. We need to set a trap so we can see how far up the chain they are and then decide who to eliminate so we can shut down the entire organization."

"So, do we play a game of poker to decide who gets to tell the president that his wife is on Obsidian's payroll?"

Wood chuckled. "Is that what it would take to get you to play me again?"

"Well, it's the only way to guarantee that you would be the one to have to deliver the bad news."

"I'll have to come up with another way to get you to play me then because we're not telling him."

Blunt furrowed his brow. "He needs to know."

"I agree, but like I said earlier, I don't trust any else. Obsidian could have someone in Secret Service who could overhear something or have Young's office bugged. I'm just not willing to risk it. Right now, our biggest weapon is the element of surprise. If we can navigate these waters stealthily, we should be able to extract more intel out of this."

Blunt glanced at his phone again as it vibrated on the table. He shook his head and held up the screen so Wood could see it.

"Who is that?" Wood asked.

"That's Milton Reese, the head of the New York Branch of A Hand Up. And it's too late now to handle this investigation quietly."

"Damn it, Blunt. That's what I get for getting your team involved. A bunch of renegades and rebels who force me to clean up their messes more often than not."

"Can't argue with the results."

"I can in this case because it might just cost us a golden opportunity to start putting together an org chart of this group. Reese has been on our watch list for a while."

"What am I supposed to tell them?" Blunt asked. "They've got Reese tied up, and he's seen them. Cleaning this up would be like trying to put toothpaste back into the tube."

"I don't care how difficult of a task it is. Shut them down now."

"Okay," Blunt said. "I'll take care of it."

"I've gotta run, but I'm counting on you to handle this. Let's talk soon about the first lady."

Blunt watched Wood exit through the front door before he texted Hawk back and told him to back off Reese. Hawk quickly responded:

"That's not what I meant when I asked you how to proceed."

Blunt grunted and fired back another text:

"Make it seem like you are simply robbing him, not part of some covert ops team affiliated with the government."

He waited for a few seconds while Hawk typed his reply:

"Too late for that now."

Blunt tucked his phone in his pocket, choosing not to reply. The damage had already been done. His team would figure out a way, but he didn't want to know about it. Plausible deniability was his best response when Wood inquired about how his team handled Reese.

CHAPTER 14

New York City

HAWK'S MOUTH GAPED as he read the response from Blunt. *Back off?* Based on that message alone, Hawk wondered if Blunt had been compromised somehow and was being forced to do things against his will. Or if his phone had been stolen. Nothing made sense. Blunt never told them to back off. He was a "keep pushing forward" kind of guy.

"What is it?" Alex asked as she snatched the cell from Hawk's hands.

Hawk ushered Alex and Black to the far corner of the room to discuss their next steps.

Alex read the text in a whisper. "Are you kidding me?" she said when she was finished.

"That doesn't sound like Blunt," Black said.

Hawk sighed. "It's hard to disagree with you. The only reasonable explanation I can come up with is that he's just following orders."

"Whose orders?" Alex asked. "The head of Obsidian?"

"Randy Wood is one of the only people who could tell Blunt to pass along an order like that and he'd comply," Hawk said.

"Well, it's too late for all that," Black said. "We need to move on this interrogation of Mr. Reese if we're going to glean anything from it."

"Agreed," Hawk snapped. "And Blunt still hasn't responded to my follow-up message requesting direction on what to do next, which means he doesn't want to know what we're about to do."

"And what did you have in mind?" Black asked. "I'd be happy to pull the trigger on this traitor."

Hawk took a deep breath and exhaled slowly. "My best guess is that Blunt might not want us removing this piece of garbage because the CIA is working some angle we didn't know about."

"So we keep everything normal then?" Alex asked. "Just act like nothing happened? You think Reese is going to comply with our wishes and not signal to someone that he's been compromised?"

Hawk shook his head. "No, but maybe we keep up a ruse as long as possible until we figure out exactly what Obsidian has planned next."

"And how do you intend to do that?" Black asked.

"Just follow my lead," Hawk said.

He strode across the room toward Reese, who was tethered to a chair. Alex and Black joined, forming an intimidating line in front of their captive.

Hawk turned to Alex. "Did you message the receptionist?"

She nodded. "She's not coming back today or tomorrow."

Hawk smiled. "Good. Now we can get down to business."

Reese squirmed in his seat, fighting against the duct tape that kept him in place. "If you think I'm going to help you, you're delusional."

"I'm not going to ask twice," Hawk said.

Black reached into his pocket and pulled out a cigar cutter. He held it up in front of Reese's face so he could see it. "Do you know what this is?"

Reese nodded and shied away from Black, who intruded into the prisoner's personal space.

"This is called a guillotine," Black said, forging ahead despite Reese's response. "I'm just going to slide one of your fingers in here like so and then snip—your finger is detached from your body. Now, if you wonder how effective this device is, the last guy I interrogated who refused is now called Knuckles because that's all he has left."

"Now," Hawk said as he rubbed his hands

together, "Mr. Reese, now would be a good time to reconsider your unwillingness to help us."

Reese squeezed his eyes shut and scrunched up his nose. "Okay, okay. I'll help you."

"Good choice," Hawk said as Black snipped the end off a cigar he'd pulled out of his pocket. The sound of the metal slicing off the tip of the stogie resulted in a shudder from Reese.

"Let's get down to business," Black said. "Time to start talking."

* * *

THE NEXT MORNING, Hawk and Alex ventured back to A Hand Up's offices, while Black stayed at their hotel with Reese. Black expressed his displeasure with being a glorified babysitter, a complaint that went ignored by his two colleagues.

While questioning Reese the previous night, Alex captured his speech patterns and created a voice simulator for Hawk to use while at the office. He immediately put the device to use by telling Reese's secretary administrative assistant to take the rest of the week off with pay, an order she sounded thrilled to obey.

Hawk went to work combing through all of Reese's emails to determine what exactly Obsidian was planning, while Alex went to work digging through A Hand Up's servers to see if she could find anything of interest.

At 10:30 a.m., Hawk took a call from Reese's direct line. Alex, who was seated on the other side of the desk, started the tracing procedure.

"How are things looking on your end?" the man asked, dispensing of any formalities.

"Good so far. And you?" Hawk asked.

"Never better."

Relieved that his voice was apparently a sufficient match that whoever the caller was didn't hesitate to continue the conversation, Hawk sighed.

"Is there anything I need to know about?" Hawk asked.

"As far as I can tell, we're on target to hit all our deadlines. I don't see anything slowing us down, at least when it comes to elements that are within our control."

"Do you anticipate anything happening between now and Tuesday?"

"I don't think so. If everything goes as planned, we'll be ready to unleash the project then. Just have everything in place by Monday afternoon, and we'll be fine."

"That won't be a problem," Hawk said.

"That's what I like to hear. Just shoot me a text when you get the package so I can rest easy knowing we haven't had any delays."

"You got it. Talk to you then."

Hawk hung up and looked wide-eyed at Alex. "What package are they talking about?"

"You got me," Alex said. "But the way that caller spoke about it, I don't think he was talking about an order of pens and notepads for the supply closet."

"Did you get a trace on that number?" Hawk asked.

She shook her head. "Whoever set up the routing protocol for that man is highly skilled. Following that line had me pinging all over the world. There wasn't anything definitive I could determine."

"Are you sure?" Hawk asked, his brows arching as if he were begging for her answer to be different this time.

She nodded. "Sure as I am that I'm sitting here."

"I want to call the Chicago office," Hawk said as he glanced at his watch. "They should be in by now."

"But what if that was the Chicago office director you just spoke with? You'll be busted without a doubt."

"I can always hang up if I don't recognize his voice."

"Okay," she said. "Give me a second, and I'll scramble the location of your call."

She typed furiously on her keyboard for a minute before announcing she was ready for Hawk to proceed. He picked up the phone and dialed the

Chicago office's number. The secretary answered and patched him through to Eddie Willingham, the director of the Chicago office.

"Eddie, this is Milt," Hawk said. "How the heck are you?"

"I'd be a lot better if I wasn't freezing my face off every time I go outside."

"Maybe you should volunteer to open an office in Miami."

"I tried that, remember? Dan beat me out for it. But thanks for rubbing it in."

Hawk looked at Alex, who scowled at him. "So sorry. Forgot about how painful that was for you."

"Forget about it, Milt. What do you need?"

"Just checking to make sure I haven't missed anything regarding Tuesday's launch."

"All conditions are a go here. What about in New York?"

"No issues yet, so I anticipate everything will go off without a hitch."

"Good," Willingham said. "So, where are you going Tuesday?"

"I haven't thought about it yet."

"Well, you better. You need to take a long vacation far away just like they told us to. If not, you might regret it."

"Of course," Hawk said. "I mean, I've thought

about it. I just haven't made any concrete plans. I was thinking of maybe Fiji or somewhere like that."

"Excellent choice. Maggie and I went there for our anniversary last year."

"What about you? Where are you planning on going?"

Eddie chuckled. "What is wrong with you today? The last time you called, we talked about this. I'm heading to New Zealand for an extended trip."

"Oh, yes," Hawk said, earning another disapproving look from Alex. "I hear those Kiwis are fun. Beautiful country."

"I know. You've told me all about your trips there many times. You're the one who's convinced me to go."

"Have a nice trip. I'm sure we'll talk after we all get back."

"Of course. Stay safe," Eddie said before hanging up.

"What a disaster," Alex said. "At least if he tries to trace the call, he'll see it lead back to this office. You're lucky he didn't act like he suspecting anything. But don't worry because I pulled the plug on the rerouting as soon as I realized we were getting the Chicago office director."

"The important thing is we know something major is going down on Tuesday—and New York City isn't the only place in Obsidian's sights."

Before the discussion could continue, someone pressed the buzzer, requesting to be admitted to the building. Alex and Hawk rushed up to the front desk and looked at the man depicted on the security camera screen. He was leaning on a dolly stacked over four feet high with square boxes.

"What do you have there?"

"A delivery for Mr. Milton Reese," the man said.

"Come on up," Alex said as she pushed a button to allow him access. They both watched as he wheeled the packages onto the elevator and then entered the lobby area once he reached A Hand Up's floor.

"I just need a signature right here," the deliveryman said as he handed a tablet to Alex.

She scribbled an illegible name onto the screen and handed it back. He squinted as he studied what she wrote.

"First and last name, please," he said.

"Nancy Register," she said.

The man thanked her before ducking outside of the room and leaving the offices.

"What do you think this is?" Alex asked.

"There's only one way to find out," Hawk said as he pulled out a pocketknife and slipped it beneath the tape securing the box shut.

Hawk's eyes widened and his mouth fell agape as

he stared at the contents.

"What is it?" she asked.

"It's a bomb. Obsidian is going to attempt to set off bombs all across the country."

CHAPTER 15

BLUNT STARED AT THE screen on his phone, alerting him that Randy Wood was calling. Given their conversation from the night before, Blunt wasn't surprised. Wood needed assurance that he wasn't going to be surprised with something the Phoenix Foundation team did. And Blunt was relieved that he wouldn't have to disappoint the deputy director, at least not yet.

"Did your team return everything back to the way it was yesterday?" Wood asked.

"As far as I know," Blunt said as he paced around his office.

"Just make sure you keep a tight leash on them. We have a good plan in place to unmask Obsidian's chief players. Unfortunately, it's going to take some time, and I know patience is something Hawk runs short of."

"I'll do my best, though I'm not sure we have the luxury of taking much time."

"Just leave the speculation to us. You guys handle the field assignments we throw you and stick to the script."

"You're the boss," Blunt said, though without an ounce of conviction.

"I'll be in touch soon."

Blunt hung up and noticed Hawk had tried to call.

"What did you find out?" Blunt asked as Hawk answered his phone.

"We have a serious threat in both New York and Chicago."

"How serious?"

"Depends on where Obsidian is planning on planting this thing," Hawk said. "But we just received a shipment of materials here necessary to build a bomb. The only thing missing are the explosives."

"I'm sure they'll be arriving soon."

Hawk nodded. "I know. If we leave this office, we'll be in danger of tipping off Obsidian that we discovered what they were up to."

"And that can't happen. I just spoke with Randy Wood, and he's really nervous that we're going to torpedo his plan to uncover who's at the top of Obsidian's power structure."

"Well, we might not need a plan that takes weeks to unfold," Hawk said. "Alex has been digging around this morning on the servers here and found some interesting things. I'll let her tell you about them now."

A few seconds later, Alex's voice was coming through the speaker. "I found Obsidian's white paper on this entire project—the real white paper, not that general overview Black found at Fortner's place. Their quest for money is simply a means to an end."

"And what's their endgame?" Blunt asked.

"To control as many of the world market sectors as possible to create a more *utopian existence*."

"We already knew this wasn't just about money. But a utopian existence? Are you serious?"

Alex chuckled. "Would I lie to you? That last phrase is a direct quote. They have something else in mind for the rest of us peons."

"And did you find out what?"

"Not yet. I know it's a vague and ambiguous goal statement, but it at least lets us know that they have very ambitious plans."

"What else did you find?"

"I found out where most of the money is going—a shell corporation in the Bahamas called Apollo Corp."

"Apollo Corp?" Blunt asked. "That's rich."

"How so?" Alex said. "I always hated mythology."

"Apollo was the Greek god over many things, including both plagues and medicine. Sound familiar?"

Alex sighed. "Would they really name their fake corporation something that on the nose?"

"Probably an inside joke," Blunt said. "I doubt these arrogant bastards ever imagined they'd get caught."

"Never underestimate a man entering his second century," Alex said with a soft laugh.

"You think that's funny, don't you?" Blunt said. "If the end of the world comes soon, who would you rather be with: someone who doesn't know how to start a fire or someone who knows how to grow crops, find water, and survive on the scarcest of resources?"

"I'm with Hawk no matter what, so that's not even a hypothetical I can entertain."

"Based on what Obsidian is scheming to do, this very much might be our reality sooner than we'd like to imagine," Blunt said.

Hawk jumped on the call. "I couldn't agree more. In the past, the attacks have been more localized and specific to a region. However, this time it seems like they're planning a coordinated event."

"Do you believe this is going to be global or just limited to the U.S.?" Blunt asked.

"So far we don't have any proof that anything is taking place outside of the U.S., but you might want to put on alert those cities that have A Hand Up offices."

"If this truly is a worldwide attack, this isn't going to be easy to stop," Blunt said.

"Of course not," Hawk said. "But we'll think of something."

Blunt stroked his chin. "Keep digging. We need to know as much as we can before we start issuing warnings to every law enforcement entity in the free world."

CHAPTER 16

BLUNT TUGGED ON HIS stocking cap covering his wispy gray hair and then looked the White House security guard in the eyes. He glanced up and down between the photo on the badge and at Blunt's face. After comparing the image with the man, the guard waved Blunt inside.

He removed his hat once he entered and then hustled to the Secret Service lounge to chat with Big Earv, who was running point on President Young's detail that afternoon. Big Earv was holding a cup of coffee while checking his watch when Blunt entered the room.

"Big Earv," Blunt said as he strode inside with his arms wide.

"They will let anyone on the White House grounds these days, won't they?" Big Earv said.

"When you were here when they built the damn place, no one tends to put up much of a fuss when you ask for permission to enter," Blunt said with a wink.

"You've probably been using that joke longer than I've been alive."

"Probably—and it was just as funny back then as it is now," Blunt said as he smiled. "I really do appreciate you setting this meeting up for me."

"I still don't understand why you couldn't set this up like all your other meetings. Is there something happening that I need to be aware of?"

Blunt crammed his cigar into his mouth and chewed on the end while he responded. "It's quite possible that a terrorist attack might happen soon, but we don't want to talk about it publicly because there is a serious security breach right now within every branch of the government. Until we can identify who's leaking all this information, we have to keep our mouths shut. I trust you didn't tell anyone else, did you?"

Big Earv shook his head. "Not a soul. I'll be the one vetting the president's limo when he goes to leave, and I'll also be stationed inside. You have nothing to worry about."

"Thanks, Big Earv. I know I can always count on you."

"You did get me this job, so you know I'm always willing and ready to do you a solid."

Big Earv led Blunt downstairs to where Young's limo would transport him to a special fundraising event at the Kennedy Center.

"You won't have long to talk with Young, so just be ready," Big Earv said.

"Roger that," Blunt said before he ducked inside the limo. He waited for fifteen minutes before activity started swirling around the underground garage. Eventually, Big Earv stepped inside, followed by President Young and a couple more agents.

Young furrowed his brow when he noticed Blunt sitting in the back of the vehicle.

"Mr. President, there's someone who requested a private meeting with you," Big Earv said.

"J.D.?" Young said. "What the hell are you doing here?"

"We need to talk," Blunt said.

"You know my door is always open to you," Young said. "Make an appointment with my secretary. You don't need to be sneaking around like you're some groveling staffer."

A faint smile spread across Blunt's lips. "I appreciate the sentiment, but I wouldn't be meeting you like this unless I had a good reason to."

"What's going on?"

"Do you remember telling me that you would let my team know the truth about Shane Samuels?" Blunt asked.

Young rubbed his face with both hands and sighed. "I vaguely recall saying something to that effect."

"Well, it's past time to find out what Samuels was up to when you directed him to join our team."

"Why? Is something wrong?"

"The truth, Noah. I need it right now."

Young shrugged. "You don't think I've been purposefully keeping this from you, do you?"

"Quite frankly, I don't know what to think at this point."

"I have a country to run, you know. It wasn't all that big of a deal really."

"If it's not that big of a deal, it won't be a big deal to tell me," Blunt said before he bit down hard on his cigar. "We have some dangling loose ends that need to be tied up before we can go any further with our investigation of a few individuals. Shane Samuels is one of those loose ends."

Young slapped his thighs and took a deep breath. "Where to begin. Well, Madeline's cousin is Shane's uncle. She's known his family for years. I have a picture of him at his high school graduation. I wouldn't say he's been like a son to me, but definitely like a favorite nephew."

"What made you think he was qualified to work with my team?" Blunt asked, eyeing Young closely.

"The FBI dismissed him because of inner office politics, but before that he was one of their best agents. So, I helped him out by getting the CIA's black ops division to hire him for certain missions where they needed help. He was doing really dangerous stuff but didn't care. Shane just loved the work."

"And so that's your criteria for throwing your weight around and landing a position for someone like that? He didn't exactly possess the kind of stability you'd expect from a person in his position. To be really honest, he was erratic at times and scared me."

"But he got the job done," Young said.

"Sometimes, but at what cost? He's not the kind of person you want working for you."

"He was perfect for his assignment," Young said.

"Which was what exactly?"

Hesitating to respond, Young turned his focus outside the window of the car as it rolled through the streets of Washington.

"I'd heard Brady Hawk was a bit of a loose canon and needed to be reined in. So, I asked Samuels to help us. We needed an outside perspective on Hawk."

"We?"

"Madeline was helping me with some of those decisions at the time," Young said. "That's why I strongly recommended Samuels. I knew he was capable of doing something you couldn't."

"Which was what exactly?"

"Making an assessment without letting your emotions get in the way. Look, I get it. It's never easy to separate our relationships with our assignments. Sometimes, we just have to trust people that can survey a situation without all that emotional baggage attached."

"I'm sure you know that your last comment is bathed in irony."

"And I'm not the least bit bothered by it," Young said. "And for what it's worth, he came back to me and gave me a full assessment of your team. He said everyone serving under you are dedicated team members and wholly committed to serving their country no matter the cost."

"Next time, please give me a heads up about those types of things," Blunt said.

But that's not what he was thinking. He knew exactly who the traitor was on his team during that time—Shane Samuels. Blunt clenched his fists and contemplated taking a swing at the president. No matter how ill-advised it might've been, Blunt would've felt better about it all, even if just for a moment.

The limo pulled to a stop around the back of the Kennedy Center. Big Earv got out first, followed by Young and the rest of the secret service members.

Blunt waited until the limo parked away from the underground entrance before he exited the vehicle.

Shane Samuels was spying on Blunt's team—and

the first lady was undoubtedly behind it. Even before Blunt knew about the existence of Obsidian, it had an agent who had managed to infiltrate the U.S.'s most top secret special ops unit.

Blunt felt a wave of paranoia sweep over him. He wasn't sure if there was a single person he could trust outside his team—and that even included Randy Wood.

Once Blunt returned home, he called the team and told them what Young had said. Blunt also gave them specific instructions on how to clean up the mess in New York.

It was time to take action.

CHAPTER 17

Washington, D.C.

TWO DAYS LATER, Hawk slapped a copy of *The New York Times* down on the conference room table before settling into his chair. He was the last one to the room as usual despite Alex's repeated pleas to make a more concerted effort to be punctual.

"Would you like for me to read this aloud?" Hawk asked Blunt while pointing at the newspaper.

Blunt held his hands out wide. "By all means, I'd love to hear it."

Hawk read *Times*' reporter Camille Youngblood's report about how Milton Reese, the non-profit director of the New York City branch of A Hand Up was found dead floating in the Hudson River. The story also detailed how the NYPD worked in conjunction with the FBI to foil a plot to bomb the city's subway system. The FBI agent running point on the case said that Reese planned to act alone and that there was no reason to fear an attack.

When Hawk finished reading, he gave Blunt a sideways glance. "The subway system? How did they determine that?"

"They didn't," Blunt said. "I told the FBI what to say. We needed to eliminate Reese without drawing suspicion that we were on to them. It might make Obsidian a little more cautious, but they won't be quaking in their boots after that last piece of news."

"And Randy Wood didn't give you a hard time about this?" Black asked.

"Randy never goes easy on me about anything," Blunt said. "I had to listen to him vent for a while, explaining how we probably ruined the entire operation. But by the time he got everything off his chest, he wanted to make sure my team was still on board with stopping Obsidian's coordinated attack."

"Of course we are," Hawk said. "But unless the CIA has something that can clone us—and I'm not talking about Michael Keaton-type clones—we can't do this alone."

"We don't even know what this is," Black said. "We're only assuming at this point that Obsidian is coordinating attacks in the same cities as A Hand Up offices, yet we have no intel that states this is the case."

"There's only one way to find out," Alex said.

"And how's that?" Black asked.

"We need to go to the source himself," she said.

Blunt nodded. "Samuels?"

"Of course. He's the one out there making everything happen for Obsidian," Alex said. "He's dealing with Orlovsky, who's obviously supplying all the weapons."

"Great idea," Black said. "But if we can't draw him out, we can't confirm anything."

Alex smiled and raised her index finger. "Funny that you should say that because I actually did a little digging and—"

"You mean hacking," Black said.

"Whatever," she said with a shrug. "The point is I found the first lady's cell phone record and was able to analyze several of her calls, including one that connected with a cell tower in—you guessed it— Dubai. And on the same date Samuels was there."

Hawk cocked his head to one side. "How did you know Samuels was there at that time?"

She glared at him. "Too soon, hun."

"So, the first lady is far more than a casual observer," Black said. "She's deep into this operation with Obsidian."

Blunt winced. "God forbid she's actually running the show, but it's not out of the realm of possibility yet. Either way, she's highly involved. And her connection to Samuels is something we must exploit."

"And how exactly are going to do that?" Black asked.

"I happen to know where she meets when she wants to avoid the public eye," Alex said. "I've seen surveillance footage of her meeting with lobbyists and the like on satellite footage I obtained from the NSA."

"We can't exactly ask her to show up in some public place for our own op," Black said. "Do you have any idea on how you plan to accomplish this?"

She nodded. "Piece of cake."

"All except for the Secret Service bit," Black said. "They're not about to let her out of their sights no matter how skilled she is at sneaking away."

"I've got that covered too," Alex said.

"Then let's get to planning," Blunt said. "We only have three days before these attacks are schedule to take place."

Alex grinned. "I'm already two steps ahead of you, sir."

CHAPTER 18

Washington, D.C.

ALEX STUDIED HER FACE in her compact one more time before she snapped it shut and exited the black SUV along with her Secret Service detail. She had never been to Crispus Attucks Park, but she'd wanted to visit it for a while. And once she discovered it was one of the first lady's favorite haunts when she wanted to feel normal or talk to someone without the press hovering over her, Alex set that as the meeting place with Samuels.

She pulled the collar on her coat taut and wondered if she'd be able to dupe Samuels. Although she spent most of her time behind a terminal, she was more than capable in the field. Hawk would likely be dead if she wasn't. But this was another level of espionage that she'd never ventured to before.

"Think I can do this?" Alex asked, her voice quivering as it came through the coms.

"There's nothing to be afraid of, Mrs. Hawk," Big Earv said. "We'll take care of you. Even if Samuels figures out who you are, he's not going to try anything in a public place. And if he does, it'll be the last thing he tries to do before I snuff him out."

"Thank you for that lovely sentiment," she said. "And, Big Earv?"

"Yes?"

"Don't ever call me Mrs. Hawk again."

He chuckled. "Yes, ma'am."

"Or ma'am either. Alex, just Alex. That's more than enough."

"Sorry, Alex. It's a tough habit to break."

"Leave him alone," Hawk chimed in. "I kind of like the sound of Mrs. Hawk."

"No one asked for your opinion," Alex said with a slight grin. "I'll deal with you later."

She glanced over her shoulder at Hawk, who was sporting a coat and tie along with Black, both looking as if they were seasoned Secret Service agents.

He gave her a subtle nod, and she winked back at him.

She ambled alone until she reached a bench and settled onto the far left end. Opening a copy of *The Washington Post*, Alex took the opportunity to catch up on all the capital's gossip. There was one article ranking the wealthiest bachelors in the city.

"No wonder nobody reads newspapers any more," she muttered. "This is just like click bait headlines in print format."

"Are you reading about the most available bachelors?" Big Earv asked.

"How'd you know?"

"That's the only reason I buy *The Post*," Big Earv said. "I'm still waiting for the day when I'm on the list."

"I hate to break it to you, Big Earv, but as long as you're serving in the Secret Service, you're never going to be on that list," Alex said. "Remember, you're in the *Secret* Service. Nobody is supposed to know about you."

"But I make a good living and have devilishly handsome looks," he said.

"For a glorified body guard," Alex said.

"Don't ever call me that again, *Mrs. Hawk*."

Hawk laughed so loud that it came across the coms.

"That's not funny," Alex said. "I hear you laughing, hun."

"Sorry, I couldn't suppress it," Hawk said. "Big Earv is in rare form today.

"You're just not around me enough," Big Earv said. "This is my daily form."

"He's not lying," the other agent said, backing up his colleague.

Alex sighed. "Enough of this foolishness," she said. "Has anyone seen any signs of Shane Samuels in this park?"

"That's a negative from me," Big Earv said. "I've seen a trio of homeless men but no sign of Samuels."

"He'll be here," Hawk said.

Alex watched the agents spread out as protocol dictated. She was certain Samuels would come, if anything out of curiosity. After scanning two more articles about the city's social scene, Alex looked up and noticed a man walking toward her with his head down. He was leaning on a cane, though Alex wasn't fooled. It was Samuels.

He walked with a noticeable limp, though exaggerated. Alex didn't buy it as a legitimate injury.

"Please tell me you didn't tear up your knee playing lacrosse," she said in a whisper. "I'm warning you that you're too old to be playing those kinds of sports."

Samuels eyed her closely. "Are you okay?"

"I have a cold and lost my voice earlier this week. I hope you can still understand me."

"Understand you? Yes. Hear you? Maybe."

"I'll try to amplify my voice as much as I can without it hurting," she said.

"Thank you."

Alex pushed an index card toward Samuels and sighed.

"What's this?" Samuels asked.

He flipped it over and read the message: They are listening but can't hear us when we whisper. Samuels nodded and eased the note back in her direction.

"So, what is the nature of this meeting?" he asked, his voice barely audible.

"Good," she said softly. "Really good, in fact. I was just wondering how your family was doing."

"They're fine. No big family drama to speak of."

"And what about your plans for Tuesday?" she said as her eyebrows shot upward.

"Same as they've been for quite a while. Nothing new there."

"I just need to know where you are planning on going? Madrid? London? Paris? Berlin?"

"You already know everything you're supposed to know."

"I have a diplomatic trip planned to Europe for next week and—"

Samuels eyed her closely. "I'm beginning to wonder if you can actually hear me. You know everything you're supposed to know."

"But if I go to a place that I shouldn't—"

"Nothing's changed from the original plan."

Alex sighed. "Your favorite aunt needs to know if she's going to have a good experience during her upcoming travels. I'm not concerned with my husband. But I am worried about myself."

Samuels took a deep breath as he scanned the area. "Look, just stay away from the airports in Madrid, London, Lisbon, and Paris."

"What about Florence and Rome?"

"You shouldn't experience any discomfort in either of those cities."

"See," Alex said, still in a whisper, "was that so difficult?"

He shook his head and gazed off into the distance. "I hope you have a plan."

"For the future?" she asked.

He shrugged. "For that—and everything else. The world is unstable right now. I'd hate for you to get stuck somewhere else and caught up in the fray."

"Of course I have a plan," Alex said. "This life isn't new to me."

"Does your plan include your husband?"

She shook her head, resulting in a slight smile from Samuels.

"You always were my favorite aunt," Samuels said.

She chuckled and leaned forward. The micro tracker in her open hand was barely visible and even less so while tucked away in her palm. Without him noticing, she slipped the device into the cuff of his pants as she patted him on the leg.

"Did you have anything else you wanted to discuss?" Samuels asked. "You made the nature of this meeting sound very urgent."

"It was," she said, her eyes bugging out. "I needed to make sure I wasn't walking into a dangerous situation next week."

"You'll be fine," Samuels said. "Have a nice trip."

"Thank you," Alex mouthed to him. He smiled and nodded before sauntering toward the park's exit.

"Let's grab him," Hawk suggested. "I'd love to interrogate the little punk."

"You had your chance in Dubai and failed," Alex said. "Besides, we got everything we needed out of him. Now he's going to lead us straight to his employer."

CHAPTER 19

THE TEAM CONVENED at the Phoenix Foundation headquarters, setting up in the conference room to monitor all of Shane Samuels's movements. Blunt wheeled his executive desk chair to join the festivities. He leaned back in his chair and propped his feet up on the table, intently watching Alex's laptop mirrored onto the large flat screen affixed to the far wall.

"This must be quality entertainment for you," Alex said while peeping over the top of her computer.

"Beats watching network television," Blunt said.

"You've got a standing invitation to come over and browse through our Bollywood DVD collection for some more engaging movies," she said.

Blunt chuckled and rolled his eyes. "I can also play solitaire on my phone for two hours and even that would be more entertaining than one of those silly foreign films."

"Don't knock it till you've tried it," Hawk said.

Blunt sighed. "I already know what I'd be getting, and this is definitely better than an Indian film."

"That depends," Hawk said.

"On what?" Blunt asked.

Hawk cocked his head to one side. "If Samuels does anything of interest. He could just be sitting around all day and counting his money for all we know."

"And that'd still be more entertaining than reading the terrible translated lines of bad actors," Blunt said.

Alex shook her head and smiled. "You just don't know what you're missing."

Blunt pointed at the monitor. "It looks like you're about to miss Samuels leaving his apartment."

They all watched the dot on her computer program drift from one room to the other and finally come to a stop near the front door.

"Looks like he's about to leave," Blunt said. "We need to know where he's going."

"False alarm," Alex said. "He's staying put for the time being."

"What was that all about?" Blunt asked. "He looked like he was ready to hit the road."

"Patience," Black said. "A stakeout can't be rushed. And believe you me, if I could rush it, I would."

For the next two hours, the team watched the dot representing Samuels's tracker on Alex's screen. There was very little movement around the house. After a while, Blunt cracked that Samuels was taking a nap.

"Maybe he's watching a riveting Bollywood movie," Black said.

Alex shot him a sideways glance. "I detected a little sarcasm in that comment."

"That's why you're a super spy, Alex," Black said. "Nothing gets by you."

Blunt sighed as he stood and pushed his chair backward. "I'm going back to my office. I was hoping this little pipsqueak would freak and do something stupid, but he's apparently staying put for now. If something changes, please come and get me."

"Well, maybe he's not planning on going anywhere," Alex said. "I just dug up some records where he paid to have a state-of-the-art security system installed."

"Why else would he do that unless he wanted to hunker down there?" Black asked. "It's not like he's personal friends with the president's family or anything and has anything to worry about."

"If he's staying put, I'm inclined to believe he's not concerned about any attack being made on Washington," Hawk said.

"Obsidian wouldn't leave Washington out of

their plans," Blunt said as he stopped near the doorway. "That'd be foolish."

"How so?" Black asked.

"The idea of attacking only where A Hand Up has offices makes sense, but if they want to strike back hard at the U.S., they need to make a statement. And the biggest statement of all is going to be made right here."

"I think hitting New York and Chicago and L.A. would get people's attention," Hawk said.

"Perhaps, but the White House is the crown jewel," Blunt said. "It's the only city that not even the terrorists on 9/11 could successfully hit."

"They got the Pentagon," Alex said.

Blunt cocked his head to one side. "That's Arlington. It might as well be another planet compared to Washington. Just think how much more devastating 9/11 would've been had the terrorists managed to hit the White House."

"So, let's say they are trying to hit Washington," Alex said. "Who's going to be the one delivering that bomb?"

"Samuels," Hawk said.

"Not if he's holed up in his apartment for the next few days," Blunt said.

"Unless . . ." Black said, raising his index finger.

"Unless what?" Alex said.

"Unless he's already planted the bomb," Black said. "He'll have an alibi with that fancy security system of his and can set off the explosives from the comfort of his couch. Not a shabby plan at all."

Blunt sighed and shook his head. "And I just can't help but think he was feeding the first lady exactly what she wanted to hear regarding where the attacks were going to be. If he's smart, he didn't trust her—or Alex as the first lady—and wanted to give her something to satisfy her inquiries."

"Are you playing a hunch here?" Hawk asked.

"Does a one-legged duck swim in a circle?" Blunt fired back. "That's what I do. I hunch, and then you guys gather the intel and analyze it."

"You want us to break into Samuels's apartment, don't you?" Alex asked.

"It's like we've been working together so long that you can read my mind," Blunt said. "There's got to be something that punk has squirreled away somewhere in a desk or on a laptop. And I want it found so we can put a stop to this."

"And what about Randy Wood?" Alex asked.

"I'll deal with him," Blunt said with a snarl. "Now, you guys get going."

* * *

BLACK HAD ALREADY AGREED to grab a bite to eat with the rest of the team when his phone buzzed. He glanced at the name on his screen and announced that he'd catch up with everyone later at the restaurant. Once he found a quiet room, he shut the door behind him and answered the call.

"Took you long enough," Black said. "I thought you were beginning to lose your magic touch."

"I don't know who you're tangled up with this time, but these people are good," the man on the other end of the line said. "I've only read about this type of encryption capability before but had never experienced it first hand—until now."

"Did you crack it?"

"Sort of. I think one of the messages was actually sent in a code that would require a cipher of some sorts. But I'm not sure. I managed to extract what was sent in the raw data format, but I have no idea if it's something that's useable to you."

"Send it to me," Black said. "I'll forward it to our resident guru. Between the two of you, we just might be able to figure out what those communiqués said."

"All I ask is that you keep my name out of it," the man said. "You know I don't want to invite any more trouble. Lord knows it doesn't need any help finding me."

"You have my word," Black said. "I'll be discreet."

Black hung up and hustled downstairs to catch

up with the rest of the gang. He knew that if Alex found out whom he was working with, she might just sucker punch him in the gut. Black decided that if necessary, he'd take one for the team. Finding out what was on Fortner's phone was vital if they were going to catch him and finally start to unravel the shroud covering the faces of Obsidian's masterminds.

CHAPTER 20

HAWK STUDIED THE SCREEN on his laptop before directing his gaze toward the fifth-story floor of Shane Samuels's apartment. The tracker Alex had planted on Samuels was likely still lodged inside the pants leg cuff, either lying on the bedroom floor or in a laundry hamper in his closet. But Samuels hadn't gone anywhere. Based on Hawk's visual observations, Samuels was still walking around his condo.

"Think this plan will work?" Alex asked from the driver's seat.

"There's only one way to find out," Hawk said.

He activated his coms to test them. A high-pitched screeching noise made both Hawk and Alex writhe in pain for a moment.

"Geez, Hawk, you sure know how to make an entrance even on the coms," Black said. "I think you just blew out my eardrums."

"That's what I was going for," Hawk said. "I guess I'd consider this a success."

"Real funny," Black said.

"Are you in position?" Hawk asked, refocusing on the mission.

"Dressed and ready to go. The hottest fireman in Washington, D.C."

Alex chuckled. "*Second* hottest fireman."

"Do you always have to stick up for Hawk?" Black asked. "I mean, can't you let him fight his own battles every once in a while?"

"She's not fighting my battles," Hawk said. "She's just correcting you. But you gotta admit, if you're going to play second fiddle to someone, it might as well be me."

"I won't admit that even if my life were on the line," Black said. "I don't cop to lies."

"We'll settle this later, gentlemen," Alex said. "In the meantime, you two have a fire to start."

"Roger that," Black said.

Hawk watched through his binoculars from a half block away as Black jumped out of his EMT van and strode into the condo lobby entrance. A couple minutes passed smoke began pouring out of one of the first-floor windows and several residents fled through the front doors. Hawk directed his gaze to Samuels's floor, but he could still be seen flashing by the window every few minutes or so.

"Did you pull the alarm?" Hawk asked.

"With sadistic glee," Black said. "I haven't yanked on one of those since the eighth grade just minutes before Mrs. Rast's physical science mid-term that I hadn't properly studied for."

"It looks like most of the residents are heeding the warning," Alex said.

"Every one of them except our good friend Shane Samuels," Black said. "He's staying put, isn't he?"

"We didn't think this would be easy, did we?" Hawk asked.

"This stuffy fire-retardant suit says no," Black quipped.

"I'll get him out," Hawk said. "You just get ready to search the place."

Hawk hustled across the street toward the condo and rushed inside. His mere presence was met with a plethora of thank yous from residents fleeing the building.

If you only knew . . .

He lowered his face guard to shield his identity and raced up the stairs to Samuels's door. After knocking once and hearing no reply, Hawk shouted louder.

"Is anyone in there?" Hawk said. "There's a fire in the building, and you need to evacuate immediately."

"I'm fine," Samuels shouted. "I'm sure you guys will handle it."

"You need leave right this moment," Hawk said, setting his bag that Alex had helped engineer to hide a smoke machine inside down by the door.

But there were no footfalls nearing the door even as plumes were pushed beneath the doorway.

"Please, sir," Hawk said. "I'm begging you to come out now before it's too late."

Still no answer. Then Hawk drew back his axe and pummeled the door, splintering it in two hits. He kicked his way through and rushed inside, scanning the apartment for Samuels.

"Sir, I've got oxygen," Hawk said as he continued looking around for any sign of Samuels. "I'll help you get out of here."

After a frantic half minute, Hawk found Samuels on his balcony, staring at the chaos in the streets below. Hawk grabbed Samuels and ushered him toward the door.

"We've gotta go now, sir," Hawk said. "Your life is in danger. This building is becoming less structurally sound by the minute."

Samuels didn't budge.

"The longer we wait—"

"Okay, okay," Samuels said, ripping his arm away from Hawk's grip. "I'm coming. Just let me get my computer."

"We don't have time for that," Hawk said.

Samuels pulled out a gun and trained it on Hawk. "I say we do. Now step aside."

Hawk put his hands in the air in a gesture of surrender and moved out of Samuels's way. He strode toward his office, where he shoved his computer into a laptop case and flung it over his shoulder.

"I'm ready," Samuels said, his weapon still aimed at Hawk.

"Can you put that thing away?" Hawk said. "That won't be necessary."

Samuels tucked the gun into his pants and started walking toward the exit. Hawk took Samuels by the arm and led him to the hallway before pricking him with a tranquilizer needle that knocked him out in a matter of seconds.

Scooping up Samuels, Hawk raced downstairs. The concoction only lasted ten minutes, which was cutting it close for the amount of time Alex would need to get the necessary information off the laptop.

When Hawk hit the sidewalk, he rushed Samuels over to another paramedic van that had just arrived on the scene.

"This man needs some attention," Hawk said, handing off Samuels.

Then Hawk sprinted over to Alex, who was waiting in their vehicle nearby. He ripped the computer out of the bag, handing her the device along with Samuels's cell phone.

"Time to get to work," he said.

She tagged Samuels's phone with a micro tracker before taking the computer and typing furiously. Using an algorithm she wrote to break the password, she initiated the transfer of all his files over to her hard drive. Hawk nervously paced around, waiting for her to finish.

"Come on, come on," Hawk said. "He's starting to wake up."

"Almost there," she said.

"He's sitting up," Hawk said. "I need it back right now."

"Done," Alex said as she disconnected the two devices and handed the computer back to Hawk. He shoved it into place and hustled to the paramedic vehicle tending to Samuels.

"Wha—what happened?" Samuels asked.

"You passed out, sir," the paramedic said. "Smoke inhalation."

"But I—where's my laptop?"

The two men looked around but didn't see it upon a cursory glance. But Hawk, who had slipped into the van from the front seat, pushed the bag into plain view just beneath the stretcher holding Samuels.

"Oh, here," the paramedic said. "Is this it?"

"Yes, thank God," Samuels said, clutching it tightly. "Did anyone else touch this?"

"No, it was right here the whole time."

"Good," Samuels said. "I need to get going."

"But, sir, I'm not done checking you out yet."

"Yes, you are," Samuels said as he hopped down and walked away.

Hawk breathed a sigh of relief from the front passenger seat once Samuels vanished. The paramedic turned and looked at Hawk.

"Did you know that guy?" the paramedic asked.

Hawk shook his head.

"Strange dude," the man said.

Hawk seamlessly wove his way into the now growing number of first responders crowding the street. He went inside and acted as if he was making a sweep of the first floor.

"The fire's out," Black said over the coms. "Time to get out of here."

He'd barely finished talking before Alex's voice followed.

"Uh, guys, Blunt was right," she said.

"About what?" Hawk asked.

"About everything," Alex said. "Obsidian isn't going after the airports. They're going for a much higher body count—and more chaos than we might have ever dreamed possible."

CHAPTER 21

BLUNT LUMBERED INTO the Phoenix Foundation conference room and stared at the monitor on the far wall. He preferred his Sundays to be restful, but instead here he was leading a meeting just after the break of dawn. The rest of the team was already seated around the table, waiting for Alex to finish pushing all of her data onto the screen. Blunt leaned against the wall before digging in his pocket for a cigar.

"Never ignore a hunch," he said. "You have them for a reason."

"Are you going to light up that thing?" Hawk asked, gesturing to Blunt's stogie.

"Being right about something isn't necessarily the kind of victory I like to smoke to," Blunt said. "Maybe I'll fire this Cuban up after we eradicate Obsidian."

"You might be waiting a while," Black said. "These guys aren't going to go down easily."

Alex slapped the table, signaling she was finished. "It's all there now."

Everyone turned their attention to the information projected from her computer. A map of the world was dotted with locations marked for planned attacks by Obsidian along with an estimated casualty count. Instead of targeting airports, Obsidian planned to hit metro subway systems all over the globe.

Hawk's mouth fell agape. "A hundred thousand people in all these places? That's insane."

"And locations easier to bomb than airports, too," Alex said. "The security level at most international hubs has been there for a while, but the subway system? No metal detectors, easy to trap thousands of people at once, and only one way out."

"Were you able to get any specific details about how Obsidian was planning to carry out these attacks?" Blunt asked.

Alex nodded. "There were several documents offering an analysis of how to achieve the highest casualty rate while also not inviting law enforcement scrutiny."

"And what did you find?" Blunt asked.

Alex typed on her keyboard before another image appeared on the screen. "They're going to borrow something from the Nazi playbook and gas the commuters."

"Gas them?" Black asked.

"The idea is to set off bombs in strategic areas, trapping trains inside the tunnels near the platforms with a series of explosions. When the people attempt to flee the area, more explosions will occur near the exits, forcing pandemonium. Then the gas will be administered through a synchronized system of dispensers attached throughout the station."

"This would be horrific," Hawk said.

"Agreed," Blunt chimed. "The attacks during 9/11 made us genuinely mistrust others as we questioned the safety of the airline industry. For millions of people around the world who rely on this type of transportation to get to work, it's going to grind the workforce in so many of those major cities to a standstill. Not to mention, it will jumpstart a whole new cycle of fear in the public transportation sector."

"And I would bet you anything that Obsidian also has a substantial investment in technology that would be able to quickly detect weapons designed for a mass transit system," Blunt said. "Alex?"

She winked at Blunt and flashed a new slide on the screen. "Already ahead of you on this one. Micronics Industries just released a new prototype last week at Safety Expo in Chicago. It's a complete body scan that takes less than a second. The technology is light years beyond what airports are currently using.

And of course, I managed to find two major investors believed to have connections to Obsidian."

"They're going for a two-for-one approach here," Blunt said. "They're going to capitalize on the stock market swings as well as send their Mircronics stock soaring."

"We're going to need a lot of help on this one," Alex said.

"I'm on it," Blunt said as he stood. "Alex, I want you to keep digging through these files. Hawk and Black, I want you two staking out Samuels's building. It's time to bring him in for further questioning and find out what else he knows. But do it discreetly."

"Roger that," Hawk said before Blunt dismissed the team.

He returned to his office and dialed Randy Wood's number.

"We need to talk," Blunt said after Wood answered.

"What'd your team find?"

Blunt sighed. "It's worse than we imagined. We uncovered Obsidian's plans through Samuels's laptop."

"You went after him?" Wood said. "I thought I told you—"

"Don't worry. He never even knew we had possession of his computer. It was just long enough for us to extract some very meaningful information off of it. I know you've got some plan to uncover the very top of Obsidian, but we don't have time for that now. On Tuesday, they're going to strike and kill thousands upon thousands of people if we don't do something to stop them."

"What's their plan?"

"Metro railways all over the world. Trap the people during rush hour and then unleash a chemical gas on them that will kill them all. It won't be pretty."

"Are they doing that on U.S. soil?"

"I'm afraid so. Right now we know that New York and Chicago are in Obsidian's sights. And we believe there could be more. We're still trying to collect the intel and make the most informed decision."

"Fine," Wood said. "We can't let Obsidian unleash that on us, but it might cost us more time."

"I know. It's not ideal, but it's the right thing to do."

"Send over the details, and I'll contact Scotland Yard and Interpol and enlist their help."

"Thanks," Blunt said. "I'll get all that over to you shortly, but please be judicious in who you give this information to. Obsidian has eyes and ears everywhere."

Blunt spent the rest of the day poring over reports and scuttling over the important items to Wood for his analysts at the CIA to assess for additional threats. It was getting late when Hawk and Black contacted Blunt to let him know that they were going to retrieve Samuels.

"Thanks for the heads up," Blunt said. "I'm going to settle in for the show."

* * *

HAWK LOOKED THROUGH his binoculars in an effort to see any activity taking place inside Samuels's apartment. With the shades drawn, there was no way to verify the target's presence inside. However, Samuels's silhouette flitted by the windows every so often, enough to convince Hawk that the man was still inside.

"He's in there," Black said. "That much is clear."

"You can never be sure until you get a visual," Hawk said.

"Nobody else has gone in or out of that apartment since Samuels returned after our staged fire. How else could he have escaped?"

"I don't want to go up there until we know it's him," Hawk said. "It could be a trap."

"Or we could be sitting out here jawing all night while he puts the finishing touches on setting up this big attack. I say we grab him now. Besides, I don't want to spend all night out here. It's getting really cold, and I can barely feel my fingers."

"You know, there are these things called gloves

you could wear. They're a relatively new piece of technology, but word on the street is that they do a great job of keeping your hands warm."

"If my hand didn't feel like a piece of glass and I wasn't afraid it was going to shatter if I hit you, I'd punch you right now."

Hawk huffed a soft laugh through his nose and shook his head. "You know what your problem is? You're too soft. Whining over cold hands. It's a good thing Blunt doesn't send you to the desert very often. You wouldn't last one night there."

Black shot Hawk a sideways glance. "Are you done?"

"Do you want me to be?"

"Let's just go get our guy."

The two men got out of the car and ascended the building to Samuels's floor.

"Alex, are you reading all of this?" Hawk asked in a whisper.

"Loud and clear," she said. "Your body cams are coming in perfectly."

"Great," Black said. "Let's go get this sonofabitch."

Hawk affixed the silencer to the end of his gun and blew the lock off in one shot. Black kicked the door in, and the two men fanned out across the apartment in search of Samuels.

As Hawk eased into the living room area, a shadowy figure caught his eye. He swung around to his left to shoot and noticed it was a cardboard cutout situated on an automated vacuum cleaner that was roving around the living room.

"Damn it," Hawk said. "He pulled one over on us."

"No kidding," Black said, holding up a piece of paper he'd snatched off the kitchen counter. "Get a load of this."

Hawk walked across the room and read the note. In the lower right corner, the microdot tracker was affixed to the page with a piece of tape. "Nice try," were the only words scrawled in Samuels's handwriting.

Hawk winced as his ears were pierced with the sound of Blunt launching into a string of expletives.

"Now what do we do?" Black said as he shook his head and looked at his partner.

"The only thing we can do—pray."

CHAPTER 22

HAWK WANTED TO SKIP the act of drinking coffee and inject the caffeine directly into his veins. He squeezed his eyes shut and opened them again, hoping that the act would serve as a physical reboot for his body. But nothing changed. All the activity from the night before along with the combination of long hours trying to bring down Obsidian had left his tank nearly empty.

"Eat," Alex said, shoving a bagel loaded with cream cheese in front of him.

Hawk looked up at her and furrowed his brow. "Alex? Is that you?"

She rolled her eyes. "You're tired, but I have a feeling you're still capable of deadpanning some joke you think is funny."

Hawk ignored her comment, knowing he was about to prove her hunch correct. "I had no idea you possessed such maternal instincts. Forcing boys to eat and telling them they're not eating enough are two things mothers do best for their sons."

"I'm glad I could once again deliver shock and awe to you in the humblest of forms," she said with a sneer. "It's just a bagel. Put it in your mouth and eat it."

The edges of Hawk's lips curled upward, and then he opened wide. He wasn't even done chewing his first bite before he flashed double thumbs up signs to her.

"This is so delicious," Hawk said.

"And here's a coffee for you as well," she said as she slammed a cup onto the table next to his food.

"Aww," Hawk said. "You thought of everything. I've never seen this side of you."

"Shut up about it or I'll deliver a throat punch while you still have your mouth full."

Hawk swallowed and ate the remainder of his breakfast in silence. He had just finished with Blunt slipped into the room, toting an armful of folders.

"I've got some good news," Blunt said.

"About time," Black said. "We need to hear some after last night's debacle."

Blunt set the documents down, which cascaded across the table. "I just got a call from one of my contacts at Interpol. Law enforcement in London and Madrid were able to identify explosive devices after evacuating both subway systems last night. The bomb sweep was comprehensive, and officials are convinced they were able to uncover every device. They're also trying to keep this out of the news in order to catch the bombers."

"Good luck with that," Black said.

"I know," Blunt said. "That's why we have to be prepared for anything here. The strike isn't supposed to happen until tomorrow, but we have no idea how this might effect their plans and make Obsidian's brass change course."

Blunt's phone buzzed with a text message. He picked it up and read the note aloud: "Explosives have also been found in Paris and Frankfurt. Both metro systems have been swept clean."

"That's great news," Alex said. "Now we just need to hear about how our people are doing on this side of the Atlantic. Any word yet from New York and Chicago?"

Blunt shook his head. "Still waiting to hear from them."

Hawk's phone rattled across the table. "It's Big Earv," he announced. "Let me take this outside."

He hustled out of the room and answered the call. "What's going on?"

"I thought you might want to know that the first lady is meeting with Samuels right now," Big Earv said.

"You need to grab him."

"I can't do that. I don't have a justifiable reason."

"Go with the idea that her life might be in danger," Hawk said.

"But they're family friends."

"So what? Don't you know that one in five homicides is committed by a family member? We just need a reason to apprehend him."

"If I try to grab him now, the first lady will have me fired immediately and order the other agents to detain me."

"I'm sure you work with reasonable people."

Big Earv grunted. "You seriously don't understand the type of person who applies for a job with the Secret Service, do you? Reasonable isn't in their vocabulary. There's only one part of the job that matters—and that's protecting the asset. If the first lady says I'm endangering her by detaining someone she's meeting with cordially and there's no proof of a threat, I'm done. No one will back me up."

"Grab him, and I'll help you sort it out later."

"I just can't—but maybe you can. We just got to the first lady's favorite park. If you hurry, maybe you can detain Samuels yourself."

Hawk sighed. "Okay. I'll be there as soon as I can. And if you won't arrest Samuels for me, can you at least eavesdrop on their conversation?"

"That I can do."

"See you in a bit."

Hawk rushed back into the conference room and rehashed his conversation with Big Earv. "I'm heading out to the park. Black, I need you to come with me."

Black nodded and then followed Hawk out to the car.

"We're wading into some unprecedented waters here," Hawk said as he navigated the gridlocked streets of Washington. "The first lady as an Obsidian recruit? Who would've imagined such a thing?"

"The president still doesn't know, does he?"

Hawk shook his head. "I'm not sure he would believe it either. And if she's working with Samuels, it's the perfect cover since they're related."

"Maybe they're more than that," Black suggested.

"I guess it's possible, but she's like twenty years older than him. I've read that she treats him like the son she never had."

Black shrugged. "Still doesn't mean it's not a possibility."

"Either way, she's in deep and positioned perfectly to manipulate the president to do exactly what Obsidian wants."

A few minutes later, Hawk pulled up to the park. He and Black scanned the area for any sign of the first lady or the Secret Service.

"Are you sure this is where Big Earv told you to meet him?" Black asked.

Hawk nodded. "This is the only place she meets people in public. They must've left already."

Convinced that the park was empty, they trudged to the car. Hawk ignited the engine with the push of a button and turned on his radio.

"In breaking news, sources tell our department that, today, law enforcement officials in both New York and Chicago have foiled a terrorist plot designed to blow up busy rail transit areas."

"And the confirming text from Blunt," Black said as he held up his cell phone.

"Well, if Obsidian didn't know we were on to them before, they do now," Hawk said. "But Samuels is still running free. And who knows what he's cooking up with the first lady."

They rolled along the surface streets of Washington, listening to a report of so-called security analyst experts debate the meaning of the attack and speculate on who was behind it and why.

"Doesn't it make you want to just punch these guys in the face?" Hawk asked.

Black nodded. "It's why I don't listen to this crap. Because that's all it is: a hot, steaming pile of garbage foisted on the American public as some strange form of entertainment."

"When you keep your standards low, you're rarely disappointed," Hawk said with a smirk.

Black buried his head in his hands. "Can we please turn this off?" He paused. "No, actually, I'm demanding that you turn this off right now before I shoot up your radio."

Hawk chuckled as he turned the power off. "It's a good thing you became an operative instead of a politician."

"I would've taken a flying leap off the top of the capitol building by now," Black said.

"But knowing your luck, you probably would've survived."

"No, that's definitely good luck to survive, even in a situation as dire as that. No good luck for me, remember?"

Hawk was mulling over which of his two smart ass phrases to respond with when his phone buzzed.

"It's Big Earv," Hawk said. "Maybe he can tell us where the hell they went."

Hawk wondered what could've taken so long for Big Earv to update him on the whereabouts of the first lady and Shane Samuels.

"I was beginning to think you'd abandoned us," Hawk said as he answered.

"I'm sorry about that," Big Earv said, his voice somber.

"What's wrong, man?" Hawk asked. "You don't sound right."

"Meet me at the Dacha Beer Garden in a half hour. We need to talk."

CHAPTER 23

HAWK APPROVED OF BIG EARV'S appointed meeting lunchtime location. A sprawling outdoor space with the constant ambient hum of conversations and random dogs barking in the beer garden made Dacha a great place to have a private conversation without looking like it was a secretive one. Hawk ordered a seltzer water and a sandwich while waiting for the Secret Service insider to arrive. After a five-minute wait, he ambled up to their table and took a seat.

"Sorry about being late," he said. "I had to fill out some additional paperwork for my supervisor after our meeting this morning changed venues."

Black waited for a moment before joining them.

"Where did he come from?" Big Earv asked.

"Black had to make sure you weren't being followed," Hawk said.

"You guys are a little paranoid."

Black shook his head and scanned the area. "If we aren't, we're as good as dead."

"So tell us what happened," Hawk asked. "They changed locations on you?"

Big Earv nodded. "Less than five minutes after we arrived, Samuels demanded she relocate to another destination. He was concerned that someone knew her favorite spot and had tried to dupe him with a lookalike."

Hawk cursed under his breath. "I thought Alex was a dead ringer for the first lady."

"Yeah, well, Samuels asked her if her voice had gotten back to normal, and her response tipped him off that someone had tried to play him. Fortunately, he didn't seem to recognize me or the other agent working both details."

"So, were you able to hear what they were talking about?" Hawk asked.

"I bugged her purse so I could listen in," Big Earv said.

"And?" Black said.

"Well, at first it wasn't easy to figure out what they were talking about," Big Earv said. "They just spoke in a very cryptic code. But the longer they chatted, the more they let their guard down and I figured out what they were talking about."

"What was that?" Hawk asked.

"In short, Samuels is going to help the first lady do something," Big Earv said.

"Do what? Are they . . ." Black said before pausing and staring blankly around the patio.

"I couldn't hear everything as there was some strange interference during part of the conversation, and I'm not exactly one to go starting rumors," Big Earv said. "But there was something about the way they looked, like they were more than just family."

"Let me get this straight," Black said. "You believe that the first lady and Samuels are somewhat of an item?"

Big Earv shrugged. "I don't know what to think. But all I know is that I got a weird vibe while they were talking."

"Was there anything specific you were able to glean from their conversation?" Hawk asked.

"Samuels warned her to be nowhere near the White House tomorrow. Apparently, he's helping coordinate an attack on the presidential mansion."

Black snapped his fingers. "That's what Obsidian really cares about, isn't it? I mean, the optics of gassing thousands of commuters worldwide at the same time in major metropolitan cities in Europe and the U.S. would be great. But a single strike against the White House would be a major blow against this country. It'd destabilize every market and give them a chance to move in under the guise of night, so to speak, and seize control where people are ready to cede it in exchange for the feeling of being safe."

"Samuels didn't give you any clues as to how they intended on accomplishing such an attack, did he?" Hawk asked.

"None whatsoever, just that it's happening," Big Earv said.

"And you heard the entire conversation?" Hawk asked.

"Not everything. Like I said, there was a point near the end where I got some interference. Not sure where it was coming from, but I heard everything but the last five minutes."

Hawk finished off his seltzer water and set it down in front of him. "You should've arrested him right there."

"For what?"

"For conspiring against the United States of America, that's what," Hawk said.

"But I didn't record the conversation, only listened on it," Big Earv said. "And if I tried to accuse her of such a thing, she'd fabricate something criminal against me, and my ass would be in jail before I could say Jack Frost."

Black shook his head. "I would've shot the bastard on site."

"That's why I'm in the Secret Service and you're an assassin," Big Earv said. "There are some problems that are only exacerbated by killing a person."

Black set his jaw. "Samuels wouldn't be one of them."

"I appreciate your patriotism, but if I made such an accusation against Samuels, you'd lose your man on the inside and you'd have no idea what was going on in the hallowed halls of the White House."

Black drew a deep breath and was about to start talking before Hawk placed hand on his colleague's arm and gave him a knowing look.

"I think what my partner is trying to say is that we appreciate what you were able to give us," Hawk said. "We're going to go after Samuels and do our best to make sure no attack on the White House happens tomorrow. You've been an amazing help, and I feel like I must buy you a drink."

Big Earv smiled. "Since I'm off duty right now, I won't refuse your generosity."

Hawk signaled for the waiter and ordered Big Earv a beer. The three men chatted for a few more minutes before Hawk looked at Black and suggested that they needed to get moving.

"What are you going to do now?" Big Earv asked.

"I'm not sure," Hawk said, reaching out to shake Big Earv's hand. "But I'll let you know as soon as we know something."

Hawk forced a smile as Big Earv strode along the sidewalk.

Black turned toward Hawk. "You know exactly what you're going to do, don't you?"

Hawk grinned. "Of course I do. We're going to tell the president."

CHAPTER 24

BLUNT WAVED AT THE GUARD manning the security station just outside the White House gates. With a faint smile, Blunt held up his security badge for the man to study it. Scanning a list of names, he identified Blunt and returned his credentials.

"Mr. Blunt, you'll need to leave that cigar right here," the guard said. "There's no smoking on the White House grounds."

"Don't worry, I only chew on these things," Blunt said with a wink before he turned and ambled inside.

Blunt entered the west wing and descended to the private area below the main floor where the president conducted all his confidential conversations. While Blunt had visited the room many times in the past, he'd never been this nervous. It was one thing to deliver a grim report about the aftermath of a terrorist attack. But to inform the president that the one person he probably thought he could trust the most was sabotaging him and feeding intel to the enemy? There would be several stages of grief exhibited before he would believe it—and then he could become a loose canon. As Blunt mulled it over, he wondered if the CIA already knew that the first lady was a spy for Obsidian, and Randy Wood didn't want to inform the president because he would leak the intel to her."

Maybe I'm overthinking this.

Blunt trusted his hunches most of the time. And if he was right about this one, he considered that he might be about to shove a wrench into the CIA's plans.

He pulled out his phone and texted Wood.

You knew about the first lady, didn't you?

Then came the reply.

Sorry, we couldn't risk you telling Young and blowing our operation.

Blunt hammered away furiously.

Too late now. Young must be read in so we can stop the impending attack on the White House.

His phone buzzed with a reply from Wood:

Don't do it!

Blunt turned his phone off and slipped it into his pocket. Wood and the CIA had a chance to put a stop to this, but letting Madeline Young carry on without at least a threat allowed Obsidian to be on the cusp of terrorizing a nation even more so than how 9/11 did. Watching office towers crumble in a massive metropolitan area struck fear in most Americans, but to have enduring images of the White House smoldering in ashes after an attack? That would wreak havoc with the country's collective psyche, possibly to an irreparable point.

Blunt took a seat in the room and waited for Young. After five minutes, the president appeared, escorted inside by a pair of Secret Service agents. The two men exited, leaving Blunt alone with Young.

"What's this emergency all about?" Young asked. "I thought Homeland Security sniffed out those two threats in Chicago and New York. Are there others that weren't in my briefing?"

Blunt's face fell as he looked down at his feet. "There's one we just found out about."

"Where? L.A.? Dallas? Miami?"

"Washington," Blunt said. "And to be quite specific, the White House."

Young scowled. "This is the most secure place in the world, you know that. I know you have to take these things seriously, but these grounds are virtually impenetrable."

"Not if no one suspects you."

Young cocked his head to one side. "You're suggesting that it's going to be an inside job, aren't you?"

Blunt nodded. "I'm not really suggesting anything. I'm telling you that someone very close to you is plotting an attack tomorrow."

"Is it one of my advisors?"

"Sir, I hate to be the one to break it to you like this, but it's Madeline, your wife."

Young laughed and shook his head. "You're joking right?"

"I wish it all was a lie, but I'm afraid it's not. I verified this information myself."

"Oh, come on, Madeline is a patriot. She'd never do anything like that."

"I have sworn affidavits from a couple of the men in the Secret Service if you still don't believe me."

"Someone must be blackmailing her," Young said. "Madeline wouldn't conceive of such an idea on her own. That's the only way that makes sense."

"It's perhaps more personal than you can comprehend right now."

"What do you mean?"

Blunt sighed. "We think she's romantically involved with someone."

Young furrowed his brow and drew back. "Think or *know*?"

"You know I always shoot you straight, sir, but the signs are all there."

"Who's she with? Is it one of my younger aides? My advisors? A cabinet member? You must have some sort of an idea."

Blunt shrugged. "We can't say for sure, but we're confident there's someone."

"Why are you telling me this?"

"Your country needs you, sir," Blunt said. "Probably more than ever before—if not for the republic's sake, for your own. We need to find out all the details if we're going to stop this before tomorrow."

"What do you need me to do?"

"I need you to clone Madeline's phone. Think you can make that happen for us?"

Young moaned. "That damn phone. She sleeps with it under her pillow. I can't get her to put it down for hardly more than a couple minutes at a time. Who knows what she does on it all day."

"That's what we'd like to find out. You just need to separate her from it for about five minutes, which is how much time we need to extract vital information to make a working replica."

"That's going to be a monumental task," Young said. "She's always on social media, sharing moments and images with her massive group of followers, tweeting out ridiculous inane things that happen here at the White

House. It makes me feel like my time in office is more like a reality TV show. And I'll tell you what. If I could ban social media, I would. It's what's ruining this country."

"I'd drop everything I was doing to help you campaign if I thought this could be a reality."

Young chuckled. "It's a pipe dream. But I'm sitting in the Oval Office, so who knows what can happen."

Blunt patted Young on the back and handed him a phone. "I'll have someone on your team connect with Alex. She'll walk you through how to clone it. And don't worry: that phone is already turned on."

A faint smile crept across Young's lips. "I can handle it."

"For what it's worth, I'm sorry to have to break this news to you."

Young shrugged. "It's all right. I've felt this was coming for a while, though I didn't think she would cheat on me. It's probably my fault anyway. These things happen when you put your ambitions ahead of your family, right?"

Blunt shook his head. "Sometimes they do. But I've almost forgotten what that's like. It's been so long for me. But since my wife died, my family has been my team. They're all like my kids. And I love 'em to pieces."

"That's how it should be," Young said. He glanced at the phone in his hand. "I'll get this done for you. We'll stop these bastards—Madeline included."

CHAPTER 25

PRESIDENT YOUNG HAD TO SET ASIDE grief over the loss of his marriage. He and Madeline had experienced rough patches before, but the past year had been more like a never-ending downhill run. No matter how hard he tried, he couldn't rekindle the magic of their early marital bliss and felt her pulling away at each opportunity. She hardly kissed him goodbye every morning, not that he was pining for her affection. The break had been a gradual one that he felt, but there hadn't been any finality to it—until now. And it surprised him how much it hurt.

Knowing that his wife was involved with someone else made Young physically ill. He had his share of indiscretions when it came to gambling and taking campaign donations that may not have been entirely legal. But he still held fast to the belief that his marriage was sacred ground. Yet Madeline obviously didn't share that same value.

He sighed as he wandered around the residential

portion of the White House. Madeline could often be found at gatherings promoting whatever her cause du jour was, but her schedule on this particular afternoon was surprisingly free. Outside of a long vacation, Young couldn't remember the last time he saw an entire afternoon empty on his wife's schedule.

Young ambled down several corridors and called her name. Eventually, he received a response.

"I'm in our bedroom," she said.

Young spun to his right and strode down the hall toward their room. She was sitting on the foot of the bed, trying to put on a pearl necklace by herself.

He forced a smile as soon as he laid eyes on her, noticing her struggle to latch her jewelry while keeping her hair up and out of the way.

"Would you like a hand?" he asked.

"If you want to give me one," she said. "I can handle this myself."

"There's nothing wrong with asking me for help, dear," Young said, doing everything in his power to keep from lashing out at her.

"Okay, sure. It's a little clasp you have to pull back so you can hook the two sides together."

Young worked quickly to secure the necklace. "You look like you're headed somewhere, but your schedule is empty."

"Yes, I know. I cleared the afternoon, but there's

this charity event I found out about at the last minute and changed my mind," she said. "I wanted to go, and we were able to get all the details worked out so I could."

"That should be fun," Young said. "Is it at the Kennedy Center?"

"You know I'm a sucker for anything held there."

Young noticed her phone sitting on the vanity counter but needed to draw her attention elsewhere so he could palm the device. He scanned the room for a distraction.

"Are you sure this dress is warm enough?" Young asked. "Look outside. It's so dark."

As soon as her eyes shifted in the direction of the window, he snatched the phone and slid it into his pocket.

"It's windy, but not snowing. At least not yet."

He forced a smile and cocked his head to one side. "February in Washington."

"God, I can't wait for the cherry blossoms to start blooming. It'll mean the end of this dreary season is almost here."

"Well, don't forget your coat tonight. And by the way, you look stunning."

Madeline straightened up and studied herself in the mirror. "Why thank you, dear. It's not easy to look this beautiful."

Or so traitorous.

"I need to finish up a few things in my study, but you have a nice time tonight," he said before he exited the room and headed down the hallway.

When he reached his library, he went to work. Following Alex's instructions, he plugged the phone into a small gray box that also led to the phone Blunt had given him. In a matter of seconds, the clone phone's screen started uploading the information. And it moved far slower than Young would've preferred.

The screen counted off the amount transferred: 5% . . . 10% . . . 12% . . . 14% . . . 17%.

"Come on, come one," Young said under his breath. He knew it'd only be a matter of seconds before Madeline stormed down the hall in search of her cell.

The cloning had only hit fifty percent when Madeline's heels clicked down the hall, and not in a leisurely manner. He knew the walk. It was the fast and furious pace, the kind he'd been all too accustomed to since his marriage had taken a downward turn.

As her footfalls drew closer, Young looked down at the screen. It was only at seventy percent. He took a deep breath and conjured up a way to distract her until the cloning finished. While it wasn't the best story, he figured it would be sufficient to stall her.

Young jumped when her phone rang. He ripped the cord from her phone and placed it at the edge of his desk.

"There you are," Madeline said as she entered the room. In her right hand, she held another phone.

"Is that your phone?" Young asked. "What is it doing in here? I hadn't even noticed it sitting on the corner there until it rang."

"Thankfully my assistant keeps better track of her phone than I do of mine," she said, holding up the phone in her hand. She snatched up her cell and headed toward the door.

"I would say don't wait up, but you're always up no matter what time I come home."

"Have fun, dear," Young said before he spun around in his chair and stared at the remnants of his failed attempt.

He waited until he could no longer hear Madeline's heels echoing down the White House residential corridors before calling Blunt.

"Did you get it?" Blunt asked.

"I'm sorry, J.D.," Young said. "I failed."

Blunt sighed. "Don't worry. We'll figure out something. Just be on high alert."

* * *

ALEX LOOKED AT THE TEXT message from Blunt and then rubbed her face. Without a clone of the first lady's phone, there was no way to hear what she was doing or know who she was talking to. The best Alex could do was identify phone numbers who called Madeline, but everyone that mattered would cover their tracks with a burner phone that couldn't be traced.

As Alex sat mulling over what was the best course of action to take, one of her computers on her desk beeped, signaling it was finished with an analysis. She wheeled over to the terminal and pecked on the keyboard to view the full report. Ever since Black had given her Fortner's phone, she'd been trying to hack it and find out what was inside. Finally, the process was finished—and she had cracked several encrypted files that Black's expert couldn't.

Alex smiled a wry grin and dug into the messages. Her mouth fell agape as she read the once-ironclad messages. Over the next fifteen minutes, she called in a few favors and compiled some more information based off what she'd learned. Then she dialed Blunt's number to deliver the good news.

"I didn't expect to be hearing from you again tonight," he said as he answered the call.

"I didn't either, but you're going to like what you're about to hear—or maybe not."

"What is it?"

"I cracked those encrypted messages on

Fortner's phone. Turns out she's not in some romantic relationship with Samuels."

Blunt grunted. "I was hoping for some real news instead of gossip."

"I'm not finished," she said. "The first lady has been in contact with Richard Joseph."

"That reminds me, have you finished that workup on him that I assigned to you a while back."

"Not yet. I've been a little busy with some other things. But I know enough to be dangerous."

"The first lady was talking to Joseph on the night of the State of the Union. Their message is very cryptic, some sort of code they've developed to keep away any suspicion. But I can tell it means more than it says on the surface. I'm just not sure what right now."

"You think Joseph is the one the first lady is involved with?"

"Nope," she said. "It's Fortner."

"What?" Blunt asked, his voice booming through the receiver. "Are you kidding me?"

"I would never do that, sir. Fortner and Madeline are quite the item. She was using the encryption program to send him racy texts. And apparently they're planning on running away together after this attack happens on the White House."

"Where does Joseph tie into all of this?"

"I'm not sure, but I just looked up his phone records and saw that she contacted him a half hour ago. I cross-referenced that with his schedule, and he's headed to some fund raising event at the Kennedy Center."

"The president told me his wife was going there tonight, too. He said it was kind of a last-minute thing."

"Well, it wasn't," Alex said. "They've been planning this for a while."

"And what are they planning?"

"I'm not sure, but if you start to put everything together, it's easy to see that this isn't about some surprise birthday party for the president."

"That's for sure," Blunt said. "Keep digging. We need to know what we're about to wade into here, and I'll call Hawk."

CHAPTER 26

MADELINE YOUNG REMOVED her pearl necklace as she got ready for bed. Staying on her feet all day and most of the evening at the fund raiser had exhausted her. She couldn't imagine just how tired she would be had she stayed until the end. But she needed to leave a little early for other reasons.

When she married Noah Young, she was enamored by his winsome personality and handsome appearance. A commanding voice with a chiseled jaw line and blue eyes that twinkled when he smiled drew her in. But his ambition and drive were what made her think she'd found her soulmate. She needed someone who was a fellow go-getter, someone with the drive to press forward even when everyone else was saying stop. That was the mentality that earned her a spot as a fighter pilot in a male-dominated profession. And even when she retired from flying to support her husband's political aspirations, she still listened to that voice in her head that challenged her to keep moving.

But he stopped listening a long time ago.

Madeline supported his dreams only because she had a few of her own, ones that she knew wouldn't likely get accomplished without wielding the power of the wife of a famous Washington politician. But her goals had changed. No longer was she interested in dedicating the rest of her life to raising the literacy rate across the globe or eradicating human trafficking, though she still believed them to be worthy causes. She wanted something for herself. While living in the midst of the capital's chaotic state, she realized she needed attention from someone who loved her, someone who cared about her, someone who saw her. And someone who she could escape with to a far away island and live a lavish lifestyle in anonymity. And Noah Young was no longer that someone, nor was he ever going to be capable of it.

Madeline tried to engage him in conversations that didn't consist solely about work. But matters of the heart were glossed over, pushed aside to discuss the latest slight from a senator from the rival party or his newest policy idea. While at the height of her fame as a pilot, she enjoyed basking in the spotlight as well as the freedom to vanish into the shadows. Such a rhythm never took place as the first lady.

What was I thinking?

In a moment of clarity, she realized she wasn't

thinking; rather, she was bewitched by Noah. However, she never imagined that his traits would eventually lead him to the White House. Yet here they were—and Madeline couldn't wait to leave.

"Noah," she called, "are you ever going to come to bed?"

Young trudged back into the bedroom. His tie was loosened along with the top button on his white oxford shirt.

"You look tired," she said.

"It's been a long day," he said. "And it's not over yet."

"What's keeping you up tonight? Is it that summit next month in Copenhagen?"

He shook his head. "It's nothing to worry about, but I'm supposed to meet with Richard Joseph in fifteen minutes."

She scowled. "What on earth for at this time of night? Can't he meet you during normal hours?"

"This is Washington, honey. There's no such thing as *normal hours*."

"Fine," she said as she rolled over and pulled the covers taut. "But before you go, can you get me a drink of water? Talking to all those people tonight has left me really parched."

"Sure," he said before spinning around and leaving.

Madeline had to make sure there was no chance

that he would walk in on her. And with the time it took for him to meander down the hall and get a drink, she'd be able to scramble up onto the dresser and affix the explosive device just like Shane Samuels had instructed her to do. By the time her husband returned, she was propped up by a couple of large pillows leaning against the headrest. Madeline forced a smile as he set the glass on her nightstand.

"Thank you," she said. "Have a good meeting, and I'll see you in the morning."

He leaned over and kissed her on the forehead before exiting the room.

She doubted she would see him in the morning—or ever again. He was always long gone by the time she got up.

This wasn't how she envisioned leaving him. She wanted to fire both canons of ammunition from a marriage full of disappointment. But in the end, this moment was perfect.

She closed her eyes and tried to fall asleep.

* * *

NOAH YOUNG WAS WISHING he was anywhere but in a meeting with Richard Joseph, the magnanimous Virginia senator. Joseph could be obnoxious and nasty when pushed on issues he believed to be important to his party. But for the most part, he was one of the few senators willing to cross the aisle to work with others for the good of the American people. Young was surprised that such a person actually existed in Washington. And it didn't take long before he counted Joseph as one of his friends.

But several intelligence briefings warned Young about Joseph, highlighting secretive meetings he held with people involved in a number of different illegal trades. Young heeded the advice, keeping Joseph at arm's length—at least he heeded it publicly. However, Young never liked being told what to do much, especially by an entire agency of people paid to be paranoid. Yet to keep the CIA and FBI brass satisfied, Young decided that he would hold any such meetings with Joseph late at night and out from underneath the CIA's watchful eye.

"Would you like a drink?" Young asked.

Joseph declined. "Not tonight. I still have some business to attend to after this."

"Keeping banker's hours, I see."

Joseph chuckled. "Only the kind kept by Washington bankers."

"You know, they called New York 'the city that never sleeps', but the Big Apple has nothing on Washington."

"It's only because everybody in this town can't sleep because of what they've done. Guilt will keep many people up late at night, tossing and turning in their warm beds while they know full well what havoc they have wrought."

"Sounds like you're all too familiar with this," Young said. "I wish I wasn't, but it's one of the hazards of living in this town."

"And that doesn't even crack the top ten list of the dangers of living here."

Young laughed softly. "Is one of those reasons you can't sleep why you wanted to meet with me?"

Joseph nodded. "It is. I made a mistake, and I need your help to wriggle out of it."

"What happened?"

Joseph sighed. "Swear you won't tell anyone, okay?"

Young raised his left hand and held it, palm out. "I swear. There. Happy now?"

"I'm never happy, but that will suffice for the purposes of this discussion."

"Just get on with it, Senator," Young said. "I'm getting more antsy by the moment."

"Okay, okay. Have you ever heard of a group called—"

Before Joseph could finish, an explosion shook the White House. Books toppled to the floor, furniture rattled across the room, the wet bar's entire glassware shattered as it fell, and a large flash of light followed by a light gray smoke filled the air.

Instinctively, Young dove to the ground and tried

to maintain his wits. The White House was obviously under attack. He never took the warning seriously, but he was wishing he had now, though he wasn't sure what he could've done differently.

After the immediate shock wore off, he tried to ascertain the direction of the explosion. When he scrambled to his feet, he noticed smoke pouring out of the residential area. Without hesitating, he raced toward it and started calling for his wife.

"Madeline, can you hear me?" Young called. "Please say something, honey!"

In the moment, he wasn't thinking about how cold she'd been lately or even the news that she was having an affair. He still cared about her and didn't want anything to happen to her.

Once he hit the section of the house just outside his bedroom, flames were raging all around him. Plumes of black smoke rolled across the floor, filling the air. Despite his best efforts to keep moving, Young couldn't move. He stumbled before collapsing to the ground.

The last thing Young remembered was hearing Joseph's voice.

"Mr. President? Mr. President? Are you all right?" Joseph asked.

Young couldn't respond in his unconscious state. And he stayed that way as a large pair of arms scooped him up and carried him away.

CHAPTER 27

HAWK AND ALEX WERE still at the office with Black and Blunt when their phones all blew up with text messages at the same time. Hawk scanned the note on his screen and slowly shook his head. He absolutely knew an attack on the White House was a possibility, but he didn't think it would actually ever happen, especially when their intel said the planned attack wasn't supposed to happen until the next day.

Blunt snapped his fingers. "Somebody turn on the television. This has got to be all over the news."

Every cable news station aired live footage of the White House, the entire residential wing ravaged by a raging fire.

Blunt slammed his fists on the table and let out a string of expletives. "This isn't what we needed. We were so close to finding out more about Obsidian."

"All isn't lost yet," Hawk said, "especially if President Young survived that attack."

"Look," Alex said, pointing at the feed crawling

across the bottom of the screen. She read it aloud: "Initial reports say that President Young survived the blast. No further details are available at this time."

"That just means he's still alive," Blunt said. "I know how this works. They don't want anyone to know if he's dead or not since that might trigger more threats."

"Where's the vice president?" Black asked.

"I'm sure he's under the full protection of the Secret Service, hunkered down in a bunker somewhere," Blunt said. "But that's not our biggest problem right now."

"I want to know how we got it all wrong?" Alex asked. "If none of this was supposed to happen until tomorrow, did Big Earv miss the most important piece of information there was?"

"That's what it looks like," Blunt said. "We need to get down there and investigate."

"You think they're going to let us in?" Black asked. "Think Randy Wood will give us the time of day now after we were off in our prediction?"

Blunt's phone buzzed and he picked it up. "Speak of the devil. Randy, I'm putting you on speaker while I'm here with the rest of my team. Now, tell us what the hell is going on."

"I should be asking you the same thing."

"Is the president okay?"

"As far as I know," Wood said. "We still don't know what happened, but we sure would appreciate your team coming down and taking a peek at the scene in case we missed something."

"It's not pretty, is it?" Blunt asked.

"I'm still driving to the White House, but it's not according to two of my agents I've spoken with who are already on the ground ready to conduct an initial walk through once the fire is quenched. They said that entire portion of the White House is burned so badly that the structural damage may take years to fix."

"Any casualties yet?"

"None that we can confirm, but it's still early. There may be people first responder teams haven't even reached yet."

"If they haven't, it's likely too late," Blunt said. "That fire looks monstrous."

"I think every fire truck in the city is on site. But as soon as I know more, I'll call you. But have your team get down here as soon as possible."

Blunt hung up and clapped his hands. "Let's get going."

The team split up, taking two vehicles. Hawk and Alex drove over together, while Blunt rode with Black.

During the ride, Hawk traded theories with Alex about how they managed to pull off the attack.

"Samuels was the one with all the weapons,"

Hawk said. "He's got to be the one responsible for setting off this attack."

"Unless he had help," Alex suggested.

"Who would help him?"

"There's only one potential suspect in my mind—The first lady. Agree?"

Hawk nodded. "If she did help Samuels, do you think she did it willingly or unknowingly?"

Alex shrugged. "The first one seems unlikely, but then again, she is a decorated military hero. It's not like she wouldn't know how to handle explosives and munitions."

Hawk's phone buzzed with a call from Blunt. Alex answered.

"Anything new?" she asked, placing the call on speaker.

"It's the first lady," Blunt said. "She's dead."

"Well, it definitely had to be unknowingly now," she said.

"Come again."

"Oh, it's just a theory Hawk and I were bandying about. Samuels is the obvious suspect here, but we would've heard about it if he got into the White House."

"Unless he got some help from Madeline," Blunt said.

"Exactly. But she'd have to be clueless about

what exactly he was doing if she wound up dead."

"I agree. So maybe Samuels was telling her one thing but planning something else without her knowledge."

"That's the strongest possibility we've come up with thus far," Alex said.

"Let's talk more when we get there. I'm not believing anything until I see her body," Blunt said before he hung up

Scores of law enforcement vehicles surrounded the White House, lights flashing and creating a constant red-and-blue strobe effect on the side building. Hawk and Alex met up with Blunt and Black before walking across the parking lot toward a woman with a bullhorn. She barked out orders as officers hustled back and forth across the grounds, complying with her orders to detain anyone trying to get a closer view.

"Someone may be trying to get back to the scene and admire their work," she said. "Don't let anyone have that pleasure without getting fingerprinted and spending a few hours in jail. Everyone understand?"

Heads bobbed up and down, signaling their agreement. A moment later, she dismissed the officers as they dispersed around the grounds.

"Are you the one coordinating all the efforts here?" Hawk asked.

She nodded. "Special Agent Amy Ingram, FBI. Who are you with?" she asked.

"We're special consultants for the CIA," Blunt said. "You haven't seen Randy Wood, have you?"

She shook her head. "About the only thing I've seen since I arrived here has been the back of this bullhorn."

"No ambulances?" Alex asked.

"Oh, there were ambulances," she said. "In fact, there were several of them, taking some of the injured people to hospitals in the area."

"Where did they all go?"

Ingram stared at Blunt. "I don't know if you're authorized to hear that information."

"Would it help if I got Randy Wood on the phone?" Blunt asked.

"I don't answer to Deputy Director Wood, so it wouldn't make much difference if you did or not."

Hawk watched Blunt clench his fists and decided to lead him away before a territorial spat erupted. This was a time when everyone needed to stay on the same side, especially if they were going to get through the night and hopefully catch the people responsible for the attack.

"Just calm down," Hawk said to his boss. "I know you don't like interagency fights. Please don't start one."

"Fine," Blunt said. "I'll see if I can find Wood."

Hawk walked back over to Alex, who was engaged in a professional conversation with Ingram.

"Hawk, there were at least four people taken to area hospitals."

"See if you can find out which one they took Young to," Hawk said.

"Why?" Ingram asked.

"Because those may not have been paramedics who rushed to his aide," Hawk said.

Ingram's mouth fell agape as she glared at Hawk. "Are you suggesting that—"

"Look, I'm not suggesting anything," Hawk said. "I'm telling you this was a pre-meditated attack and that someone may have done this to kidnap the president."

"I doubt that," she said. "All responding EMS vehicles must be approved and driven by approved personnel."

"You think that really matters in an emergency? You think that the guards out front are taking the time to examine paperwork when the president's life is on the line?"

"Well, they better," Ingram said.

"I appreciate the dedication you have to your job, but in a situation like this, security gets lax for a reason. Not everyone is going to be the stickler you are for protocol, no matter how they've been trained. This is a unique situation that is a high-stress environment.

People do things they don't normally do when they're under duress, which I'm sure you can attest to."

Alex cocked her head to one side. "Just tell us what hospitals the EMS vehicles came from."

"I can't," Ingram said. "Go talk to someone else who'll help you. But it's not going to be me."

"Have it your way," Hawk said before he turned his back and walked away from the stubborn FBI agent.

"What now?" Black asked.

"We go find the president," Hawk said. "We need to make sure he's where he's supposed to be and not in the hands of Obsidian."

"I'll drive," Black said.

"Alex, stay with Blunt," Hawk said. "Keep him sane. And when he calms down, call me and help us figure out which ambulance whisked away the president."

Hawk hustled back to Black's car, and five minutes later, they were roaring along the surface streets, retracing the path someone would've taken to reach Georgetown Hospital.

"Are you sure they would've taken the president to this one?" Black asked.

"Call it a hunch," Hawk said.

"You better be right. Because if you're wrong, it may be too late if Obsidian took him. That is what you're still thinking, right?"

"What?"

"That Obsidian snagged Young."

Hawk sighed. "I don't know if I trust any of my theories these days. This operation has been a trying one, to say the least."

"We've all been tested," Black said. "But I'm not so sure we're on a wild goose chase here."

Hawk furrowed his brow. "What do you mean?"

"I don't think Young was the target. Cultivating fear seems to be the way that an organization like Obsidian rises to power. If everyone is terrified, they'll give up things they don't need to just to feel safer."

"And Obsidian rides in to deliver on its promise to keep everyone safe, primarily by putting an end to the crime it invited in the first place."

"You have to admit that it's not a bad theory," Black said. "And there just so happens to be the added benefit of not destroying all its goodwill because the president is going to survive this attack."

"I would bet they would've preferred that he did."

Black's phone buzzed. He held it up as he responded to Hawk. "Well, the first lady certainly did survive, according to this text I just received from Blunt."

Hawk grabbed the phone from Black. "Eyes on the road," he said. After reading the message, Hawk sighed.

"That's one helluva sleeper agent," Hawk said.

"Maybe she was working with Obsidian, but not

at the level everyone else was."

Before their discussion continued, Hawk's phone buzzed with a call from Blunt.

"What'd you find out?" Hawk asked.

"Don't worry about the president," Blunt said. "He's safe and sound."

"Are you sure?" Hawk asked.

"Big Earv was the one who was in the house at the time of the explosion. He fought his way through all the debris and smoke to rescue President Young."

"Why do I get the feeling that you're not finished yet?"

Blunt chuckled. "Because I'm not."

"Okay, so what's next?" Hawk asked.

"Young did have a guest—Senator Richard Joseph," Blunt said. "Apparently, they were meeting about something when the explosion went off."

"And?"

"And Joseph is missing," Blunt said. "Hardly anyone else even knew he was here or would've thought to search for him. But several first responders saw another ambulance rushing away from the scene."

"Assuming this is Obsidian, what would they want with Joseph?" Hawk asked.

"That's what I want you to find out," Blunt said.

"We're on it," Hawk said. "But we're going to need Alex's help."

CHAPTER 28

BLUNT DISMISSED ALEX and told her the name of someone at the FBI who would help her get a terminal set up so she could assist Hawk and Black on their search for Joseph. Then Blunt walked up to Wood, who was barking out orders to several special agents working on site.

"After 9/11, I thought pretty much anything was possible when it came to attacks on American soil," Wood said as he stared at the firefighters working to assess the structural integrity of the White House. "I never would've imagined two enormous towers collapsing to the ground like that in the middle of New York City. But just when you think you've seen it all—" He sighed and shook his head before he turned and looked at Blunt.

"What has this world become?" Blunt asked. "We're seeing brazen attacks from extremists intent on weakening our government."

"And it's working," Wood said. "As much as I

respect the president, he needs a dozen more teams like yours to eliminate more of these threats at once."

"Problem is, there's only one of me," Blunt said with a wink, "and the only three agents I'd ever trust to do such work are under my direction. So, I don't know how the president is going to conjure up new operatives as good as the ones I have or even train them to a highly-skilled level, but that's a monumental task for sure."

One of the firemen shouted in Wood's direction and then signaled for him to come over.

"What's that about?" Blunt asked.

"I told them to get me when they determined it was safe to go inside," Wood said. "They got the fire out rather quickly, but we needed to make a sweep of the building for any more explosives. I'm assuming it's clear now."

Wood led Blunt over toward the fire captain managing the crews inside the charred remains of the president's living quarters.

"You sure you wanna see this?" the captain asked.

Wood nodded and looked at Blunt, who also gave an affirming answer.

"Well, follow me. I just hope neither one of you have eaten lately."

The captain took the men into the White House

and helped them navigate the smoldering ashes and toppled beams. Blunt whistled as he stopped and gawked at the hole about six feet in diameter that ripped through three walls.

"What kind of explosives were they using to do this?" Blunt asked.

"I'm not sure, sir," the fireman said. "But I believe someone on the FBI bomb squad said his unit was already analyzing everything."

They continued picking their way through the debris until they reached a body covered with a white sheet.

Wood put his hands on his hips. "Let's see it."

The captain revealed the body and immediately looked in the opposite direction. "Think that's the first lady?"

"I don't know who that is, but she must've been standing on top of the bomb," Wood said.

"Got any gloves?" Blunt asked.

Wood forked over a pair from his pocket, and Blunt slid them on. Then he knelt next to the body and gently lifted the left arm. Moving slowly to be extra careful, he slid the ring off her finger and examined the inside.

"We sure as hell can't identify her from her face," Blunt said. "We'll need a dental exam to get a positive ID, but this is her wedding ring."

Wood shook his head. "I don't know who's responsible for this, but if they thought they could win over the American public with some protest stunt like this, they couldn't be further from the truth."

"Agreed," Blunt said. "But it might be terrorists who don't give a damn about trying to change hearts and minds. They might just be satisfied to scare us all to death every day when we're driving to school or work. Simply seeding the idea that another attack might happen at any moment could be enough for them."

"Whoever did this is going to feel the brunt of an interagency hunting expedition," Wood said. "And Lord help anyone who gets in the way of that investigation."

"Ain't that the truth. We just might yet get a dozen more units like mine," Blunt said. "When President Young recovers, he's going to go ballistic and then unleash us on these pukes."

"We just need to pray that he survives."

Blunt checked his watch. "I need to pass this information along to my team. It might be useful for them soon."

Blunt dialed Hawk's number. "It's the first lady, all right."

"You're sure she's dead?" Black asked after Hawk put the call on speaker.

"I'm holding her wedding ring," Blunt said. "It's about the only thing I can identify on her at this moment."

"That bad, huh?" Hawk said.

"One of the worst I've ever seen," Blunt said. "And that includes me seeing a guy get both legs blown off just above the knee during the war."

"Glad it was you that had to verify that stuff and not me," Black said.

"I wouldn't wish this viewing on anyone," Blunt said. "And I just hope the president never sees her body like this. It'll be an image seared into his brain—and one he'll likely want to soon forget. Now hurry up and find Joseph. We need answers and fast."

CHAPTER 29

HAWK CALLED ALEX to see if she was making any headway on finding out where the missing ambulance might have gone. He and Black drove to Georgetown to learn that the president was there and in stable condition. And as evidenced by the swarm of Secret Service agents, he was also well protected. But there wasn't the faintest sign of where Joseph might have been taken.

"You found him yet?" Alex asked as she answered the phone.

"Everything has been a dead end so far," Hawk said. "We managed to identify where all the other ambulances went, and we can confirm Joseph went elsewhere based off all the information we have. So where did he go?"

"I just started compiling all the closed-circuit footage I could find," Alex said. "And I found an ambulance that disappeared around First and M streets."

"That's just north of the beltway," Hawk said. "If they jumped on that, by the time we figure out which way they went, they'll be long gone."

"That's the thing," Alex said. "They didn't get on the highway. They were very particular about avoiding it for some reason."

"So, they just vanished in that part of the city?"

"They're still there," Alex said. "I have to find them somehow. It's like a needle in a haystack."

"Now we need to burn some hay to find them."

"And how do you suggest we do that?"

"Look at all the warehouses in a five-block radius of where you last saw them," Hawk said. "Then cross-reference that with the name of people and shell corporations that rent or own those facilities, likely some transaction initiated in the past couple of years."

"I'm on it," she said. "I'll call you when I find something."

Hawk hung up and looked at Black. "Let's go to First and M."

"You think this is gonna work?" Black asked.

"You got any better ideas?"

"Not off the top of my head, but I'm sure I'll think of something."

"In the meantime, while that sawdust in burning, drive."

Black shook his head and cast a sideways glance

at Hawk. "You know we've got to come back with something."

"We will," Hawk said. "Obsidian has proven to be one step ahead of us, but whoever's running that organization is bound to slip up at some point. And when they do, we're going to be there to catch them."

Black sighed. "I'm just afraid it's going to be too late by that point. They're sliding pieces around like this is a game of chess, and we don't even know how to move or who we're playing."

"Look, I know you just wanna shoot somebody. It'd probably make you feel better for a few minutes, too. But this isn't like our typical assignments. Obsidian feels like this virus that's spreading its tentacles everywhere so it can squeeze at the right time, choking out its hosts and assuming total control. And as long as Obsidian thinks it's in control of everything, it won't see the need to squeeze just yet. We just need enough time to find the person calling the shots."

"Like I said, that's what I'm afraid of. We're going to run out of time."

"Chin up," Hawk said. "We haven't done that yet. Obsidian thinks we're playing Whack-a-Mole as we try to catch some of the lower-level operatives. But I have a hunch we're close to a big break."

Black chuckled. "Your hunches have gotten us

into trouble plenty of times lately."

"But we're still fighting, aren't we?"

Black turned the radio on as he continued to drive toward the area Hawk identified. A news anchor delivered details of the White House bombing in a somber voice, introducing a report from a woman claiming to be on the scene. She described the destruction and speculated on what happened and who may have been behind it.

"She thinks some extremist terrorist group is behind this?" Black asked, shaking his head.

"Must be her first assignment," Hawk said. "Any veteran reporter would know that this is either an accident or an inside job. No terrorist would be able to get close enough to the White House to attack the president's personal living quarters."

Hawk and Black continued to dismantle the proffered theories but were interrupted when Alex called.

"Are you there yet?" she asked.

"Almost," Hawk said. "We're about a block away."

"Good. I found something for you."

Hawk shifted in his seat and put the call on speaker. "Black can hear you now too. What did you find?"

"Almost all of the warehouses in that area have

been rented for a long time or are vacant . . . except for one."

"What's the address?"

Alex gave him directions to the warehouse before launching into an explanation of what she found. "This particular facility had been unoccupied for several years, and then six months ago it was leased by someone you might remember: Milton Reese."

"He had to be higher up in Obsidian than we realized," Black said.

"Or they were just using him as their patsy," Hawk said. "Whoever's behind all this is setting up layers of people to insulate them from the real action."

"It's smart," Alex said. "I feel like we're a one-legged duck swimming in a circle on this one so far."

"You're starting to sound like Blunt," Hawk said as he winked at Alex. "But don't worry because that's all about to change."

Their car came to a stop along the street just outside the warehouse. According to Alex, the previous owner used it as a direct mail sorting facility. But there wasn't anything she could find online or filed with the city about what Reese intended to do with the building.

Black killed the lights and the engine before both men slipped outside.

"We're here," Hawk said. "I'll call you when we know something."

"Just be careful, Hawk," she said before hanging up.

Hawk and Black stayed together, scaling a chain link fence to get inside the property. In the center was a large cinderblock building with an aluminum roof. It was as simple of a structure as anyone would find in this part of the city, which was heavily commercial peppered with a few mixed zones of residential and retail.

As they neared the building, Hawk noted a pair of security cameras positioned on the corner but no motion sensor flood lights. A pale streetlamp humming just outside the gate provided all the light in the area.

"You got your silencer on you?" Hawk asked

Black nodded. "I'll take out that light."

A few seconds later, the perimeter fell dark with only ambient city lights enabling them to see.

"Good work," Hawk said as Black returned.

"How do you want to do this?" Black asked. "Guns blazing? Or come at them from two different directions?"

"I think we need to stick together on this one," Hawk said. "We don't need to get isolated and pinned down."

"Agreed," Black said.

A row of small windows lined the exterior, set about three-fourths of the way above the ground at about fifteen feet. Hawk shimmied up a drainage pipe so he could peer inside. Most of the building was dark, but there was what appeared to be a small set of enclosed offices in the far back corner. A faint beam of light streamed from beneath one of the doors. He looked near the rollup door and saw an ambulance.

"They're here," Hawk said. "Come on."

He wedged his knife between a rubber sealant strip and the window to open it. Wriggling his way through the small opening, he eased down until his feet touched on a support beam running along the outer wall. He waited for Black and whispered instructions so they could get to the floor as stealthily as possible.

Once the reached the ground, Hawk took the lead as they approached the office. When they were about five yards away, the light turned off.

Hawk turned to Black. "They know we're here."

"Look for some cover," Black said.

Hawk looked over his shoulder toward the area that served as the staging for the direct mailers. He darted toward a slew of tables scattered haphazardly in one corner of the room, and Black followed. Before they reached safety, a shot echoed off the building walls. They scrambled behind the tables before gunfire erupted.

The shooting lasted for less than a minute before

the two combatants were hit and crumpled to the ground dead.

"We need to sweep the area," Hawk said. "Joseph is still at large."

Black tossed the men's weapons aside and emptied all the ammunition, while Hawk walked around the perimeter in search of another potential location for Joseph. Near the front, Hawk found a door with a placard that read "storage." He stopped and made eye contact with Black before pointing at the sign.

Hawk counted down, holding his fingers in the air. *3 . . . 2 . . . 1.*

Hawk swung the door open and was greeted with several shots. He dove to the ground and crawled into the room on his belly. Moving to the right, he took cover behind a shelving unit and tried to assess the situation while Black raced to the left side of the aisle.

Hawk peeked over the top of a shelf and barely got a glance before another bullet ricocheted off the wall behind him. He waited a moment before taking another look, and this time he was able to see the situation more clearly.

"We've just got one shooter," Hawk said. "He looks like he's holding Joseph hostage."

"Want me to see if I can flush him out?" Black asked.

Hawk nodded. "Do it."

He watched as Black crept to the outer edge of the shelving units on the left-hand side. They were clunky and metal, echoing every sound that hit them. Black eased down the side and disappeared from Hawk's sight. A few seconds later, a burst of shots peppered the area in front of where he had last seen the gunman—then return fire aimed in Black's direction.

Hawk eased down the righthand side until he arrived at the aisle parallel to Black. He held up his gun and motioned to it. Hawk understood the signal: Black's gun had jammed.

Before Hawk had a chance to consider their next move, he heard metal crunching against metal. He looked up to see the shelving units toppling over like a dominoes chain reaction.

Hawk preferred to stay on the outside, but he knew it would back him into a corner. So instead, he made a dash for the center aisle. However, he was clotheslined and knocked to the ground by a crowbar.

Hawk fell hard, landing on his back on the concrete floor with the iron rod clanking to a resting spot next to him. His grip loosened as his gun dropped out of his hand and slid out of reach. The attacker snatched the gun off the ground. He then stood, looming over Hawk.

"My, how our fortunes can change," said the man as he trained Hawk's gun on him.

Hawk gasped as he recognized the man's voice and then his face.

It was Shane Samuels.

"Good night, Brady Hawk."

CHAPTER 30

HAWK SET HIS JAW as he glared up at Samuels, who wore a smug smile. Hemmed in against toppled shelving units, Hawk couldn't do anything but brace himself for the bitter and painful end. A thousand thoughts rushed through his head at once, mostly about how he didn't want to leave Alex.

But in an instant, everything stopped.

The smirk pasted across Samuels's lips was replaced by twisted agony when a crowbar was lodged into the side of his head. Samuels teetered for a few seconds, dropped his gun, and collapsed on top of Hawk. He scrambled to get away from the dead body of a man who just moments before appeared menacing and on the threshold of taking Hawk's life.

Hawk had been so focused on Samuels that he hadn't seen Black reach down and pick up the crowbar. Black stooped down and offered his hand to Hawk before yanking him to his feet.

"Cutting it close their, partner," Hawk said.

Black cocked his head to one side. "I was hoping more for a thank you."

Their barb trading ended abruptly when they turned in the direction of metal scraping against the floor.

"It's the senator," Hawk said as he hurdled one of the downed shelves and raced to cut off Joseph at the door.

Hawk arrived at the same time as Joseph and pinned him to the wall with a forearm.

"What do you want from me?" Joseph asked. "I think it's pretty clear this guy abducted me."

"This guy?" Black asked as he joined the two men. "You mean you don't know him?"

"I've never seen him before in my life," Joseph said, his voice escalating several octaves.

Hawk chuckled and looked at Black. "Do you know how to tell when a politician is lying?"

Black nodded. "When his lips are moving."

"Exactly," Hawk said, returning his gaze to Joseph. "Now you're going to tell us everything."

"I was hoping you could explain everything to me," Joseph said.

Hawk grabbed a fistful of Joseph's shirt and led him outside and across the building to the other offices where he'd previously been with Samuels.

"What are you doing to me?" Joseph protested.

"Do you even know who I am? There are going to be serious repercussions for you two. You're taking a U.S. Senator hostage."

Black looked at Hawk. "Should I knock him out cold so we can discuss how we want to handle this lying sack of shit?"

"Be my guest," Hawk said as he released Joseph.

Black delivered a menacing blow that put the senator out. The two agents lifted him off the ground and placed him in a wooden chair. They secured his hands and feet and waited for him to wake up.

"You really think he's lying?" Hawk asked.

"If not, we're in a heap of trouble," Black said. "But what do we know to be true after doing this as long as we have?"

"If it smells fishy, it is fishy."

"That's right," Black said. "We don't have time to be conned by a guy who's made his living off swindling the American people in the name of public service."

"Let's wake him up then," Hawk said.

Black snatched a mug off a nearby desk and returned a minute later with a cup brimming with water.

"Would you like the honors?" Black asked.

"All yours," Hawk said.

Black splashed Joseph in the face, resulting in a disoriented awakening.

"What ha—where am I?" Joseph asked as he looked around and struggled to break free.

"You're in the same place you were when you were continuing to lie to us," Hawk said. "If it's not already abundantly clear, my colleague and I aren't big fans of blatant dishonesty. We're not too fond of politicians either. So you've got two strikes against you. It's up to you to make sure you don't reach a third. We certainly don't care for free swingers who think there are no consequences for their actions—or maybe you didn't see what happened to your buddy Shane Samuels."

"Who?" Joseph asked.

Hawk punched Joseph in the knee, eliciting several shrieks of pain. "Don't try to play us for fools. Understand, Senator?"

Joseph nodded as he grimaced in pain.

"Good," Hawk said. "I'm glad we could come to a mutual understanding for once. Now, I know based on some of your speeches in the senate that you're not a big fan of waterboarding because you think it's not a viable way to get terrorists to talk," Hawk said. "However, I must disagree with you. In my experience, it's worked wonders. But here's your chance to prove me wrong. You be honest with me and I won't resort to waterboarding. My colleague here has a really good bullshit meter. So, he'll know if you're trying to pull one over on us."

Joseph's eyes widened with fear. Hawk immediately knew he was dealing with a novice in handling a stressful situation.

"I'll tell you what you want to know," Joseph said.

"Let's start with this question," Hawk said. "How did you know Shane Samuels?"

Joseph looked down at his feet, his jaw clenched shut.

Hawk lifted his captive's chin. "I don't ask questions a second time, just FYI."

Joseph sighed. "I met him at a fund raiser. He told me that he worked for a powerful group of people who could put me in high positions if I did what they asked."

"And what did they ask you to do?"

"Nothing, at first," Joseph said. "I was beginning to wonder if the whole encounter was just some sort of hoax. But then the money started to roll in to my campaign."

"Illegally, of course," Black said.

"No, it was all legal. Small donations from Americans all over the country. Everything was aboveboard there. And quite frankly, without that money, I probably wouldn't have retained my seat in the senate."

"So they had you by the throat," Hawk said.

Joseph nodded.

"And did you meet any of these higher-ups?" Hawk asked.

"Aside from Samuels, I only knew of two other people affiliated with the group."

"Who were they?" Black asked.

Joseph pursed his lips. "One was named Milton Reese, who recently passed away."

"We're familiar with him," Hawk said. "And the other?"

"The other I met once at a charity gala in New York. This guy came up to me and told me that he was part of my funding group and said he was proud of the work I had done and was going to do."

"I need a name," Hawk said.

"Falcon Sinclair," Joseph said.

"Sinclair of Sinclair Holdings?" Black asked. "The Australian billionaire who's giving Elon Musk a run for his money on who can take tourists to the moon first?"

"That's the one."

Black whistled. "This is worse than I thought possible. Sinclair Holdings is one of the three richest investment companies in the world. If they're making a serious play to gain control everywhere, we'll all be under their thumb before we know it."

"And what was your role in all of this tonight?" Hawk asked.

"I was meeting with President Young and had a cell phone that I was supposed to dial as soon as he left the room," Joseph said as a tear streaked down his face. "I had no idea I would be setting off a bomb. If I had known they were going to ask me to do that, I would've refused."

"Spare me the waterworks," Hawk said. "You knew what you were doing was illegal, forming a partnership with some shadowy financial support group."

"But I'm not a murderer," Joseph pleaded. "At least, I never thought I'd ever be one."

"We'll let the courts decide about that," Black said as he turned off the recording app on his phone. "We've got this entire conversation on tape. Maybe it'll help with your trial because I can assure you that no prosecutor with an eye on any type of advancement is going to offer you a plea deal after you detonated the bomb that killed the first lady."

"She's dead?" Joseph asked, his face going white. "But she and I were—we were friends."

"Apparently, she was friends with a lot of people in Washington," Black said. "But it doesn't matter now because she's dead, thanks to you."

Hawk signaled for Black to step out of earshot from Joseph so they could speak privately.

"What do you want to do with this dirt bag?" Black asked.

"Let's have Randy Wood's crew deal with him. We don't need the headache—and we've got a new lead to track down."

"Roger that," Black said. "I'll coordinate this pick through Blunt."

"And I'll update Alex and see if she has anything else for us."

Hawk eased out of the office and dialed Alex's number.

"We got him," Hawk said.

"Joseph was there?"

"Along with Samuels, who was here when we arrived holding Joseph hostage. I'm not sure if it was an act or not, but we didn't really have much time to ask questions."

"So you caught Samuels?" Alex asked.

"He's dead," Hawk said. "He was about to shoot me when Black gave me a hand."

Hawk could hear her measured breathing on the other end of the line as she remained quiet.

"Are you okay? I know he was your half-brother and all."

"Yeah, I'm surprised at how I feel right now. I thought I'd be more relieved than sad, but I'm not."

"Today's been a hard day—but a good one in terms of justice."

"And you think justice has been served?" she asked.

"I know that's not really for me to decide, but we know Samuels was working for an organization that was intent on ruthlessly killing millions of people for financial gain and gaining a stranglehold on global power. It's going to be a strange time in our country the next few weeks as everyone mourns the first lady's death, too."

Alex sighed. "Yeah, about the first lady. I'm not sure she's dead."

"What do you mean? I thought the running theory was that Samuels pulled a fast one over on her and killed her with that explosion a day earlier than he said."

"That's what we thought, until now," she said.

"What'd you find, Alex?"

"I finally cracked a few of those encrypted messages from Fortner's phone that Black gave me."

"And?" Hawk asked.

"Madeline sent Fortner a message that contained a series of coordinates. And when I entered them into my mapping program, it came up as the site of the Potomac Airfield."

"Are you suggesting that she faked her death?" Hawk asked.

"I think she was in on this thing the whole time—and she's working with Fortner."

CHAPTER 31

Two hours earlier
The White House

A HAND CLAMPED AROUND Madeline Young's mouth as a masked man snatched her from beneath the covers in the residential quarters of the White House. She fought for a few seconds before he whispered in her ear.

"You have to get out now," he said. "Stop fighting. I'm here to help you escape."

The man eased his grip and released her. She twisted and turned for a moment before locking eyes with him.

"What do you want?" she said in a whisper.

"The general sent for you," the man said. "It's time to go right now."

"But I didn't—"

"It's now or never," the man said. "I mean that in every sense of the word. If we don't leave now, we're going to be killed by that bomb you set."

She looked up at the ceiling at the device with a green light blinking rapidly. "But I thought—"

"Now!" the man said, gesturing toward the closet.

She finally complied, hustling around her bed and into the spacious walk-in closet that contained a doorway leading to a secret escape tunnel. As she opened the door, another man carrying a large plastic bag emerged from the tunnel.

"Give me your ring," the man demanded as he held out his hand.

"My ring?" she asked. "What on Earth for?"

"Just do it," the other man barked. "We need to move."

Madeline twisted the ring off her finger and depressed it into the bagman's palm. She watched him drag the sack into her room and start to unzip it.

"Trust me," the other man said. "You don't want to see what's in there."

Madeline grabbed her pre-packed bag and stepped into the passage. She continued along with her escort until she left the space beneath the White House. Following her guide's directions, she wove through a series of tunnels and eventually emerged street level three blocks away from the presidential residence.

They sped along the Washington surface streets

that had quieted down for a few hours before 5:00 a.m. rolled around and the city sprang back to life at full throttle.

"Where are we going?" she asked.

"The plan hasn't changed, ma'am," the guard said. "We're still taking you to General Fortner."

She was staring toward Pennsylvania Avenue when she heard the explosion and felt the ground rumble through the car. Suddenly, alarms filled the night as fire trucks and law enforcement vehicles raced to the scene in response to the explosion. While she was still hesitant to assist in the plan, she thought she knew what she'd feel like when she was free from Noah's grasp, not that he held her tightly. That was always the problem. It was like he didn't care at all. But finally she was about to be reunited with a man who claimed that he just couldn't live without her. Madeline wasn't entirely convinced General Fortner was telling the truth when he professed the depths of his love to her. But she didn't care. It was better than her current situation, not to mention she fancied the idea of listening to people talk about her after she was gone.

They drove for fifteen minutes before they switched vehicles beneath an overpass. Instead of driving straight toward the airfield, the new car doubled back and headed toward the city.

"What are we doing?" Madeline asked as she

scooted the front edge of her seat and leaned forward. "It seems like we're going in the wrong direction."

"Just a precautionary measure, ma'am," the driver said. "We're trying to throw everyone off our scent so we can get you to the destination safely."

"You think someone is following us?" she asked.

"Not at the moment, ma'am, but any of the agencies could be tracking our vehicle using satellite imagery. We need to be extremely careful since the full weight of the government's resources are at your husband's disposal."

"You mean he wasn't the intended target?" she asked.

The other man escorting her shook his head. "This attack served a two-fold purpose, primarily for helping with your extraction."

"Extraction?" she said, furrowing her brow. "You make me sound like some CIA asset. I'm First Lady of the United States."

The man chuckled and shook his head. "Not any more, you aren't."

Madeline swallowed hard and leaned back in her seat, pondering the reality of his statement. She had grown to loathe the duties and expectations that came along with being First Lady, but that didn't mean she didn't enjoy the title. After a few minutes, she realized she had to come to terms with the fact that she had traded a title for love. Perhaps it would be the wrong choice, but there was no going back now.

Madeline and her escorts switched vehicles three times as they crisscrossed the city for an hour before finally heading to Potomac Airfield. By this time, the radio airwaves were flooded with on-the-scene reporting about the attack on the White House. Just as they pulled up to the hanger, Madeline made the driver keep the car on while she listened to one that mentioned her name.

"The explosives ripped through the residential quarters of the White House, where experts believe that the president and first lady would've been at that time in the evening," the newscaster said. "However, we can confirm that President Young survived the blast and is being treated at an area hospital. The extent of his injuries as well as his condition are unknown at this time. Meanwhile, there has been no official report on the first lady, leading to rampant speculation that she may have perished in the attack along with three other staffers in that section of the White House."

"Congratulations," the driver said as he peeked over his shoulder at Madeline. "Everyone thinks you're dead."

"That's not what he said," Madeline countered. "Did you not hear him use the word *speculation*?"

The man pulled out his phone and scrolled through a social media site. He snickered and shook his head.

"What is it?" Madeline asked.

"Everyone already believes you're dead. The hashtag #RIPFirstLady is trending right now. It worked."

"Speaking of which, we're both going to be dead if we don't get out and escort her to the general," the other guard said.

They scanned the area before exiting the vehicle and opening Madeline's door. She shuffled to the side and placed her feet on the concrete, which seemed to stretch on endlessly in every direction leading away from her location.

"Is the general here?" she asked.

One of the men nodded. "He's been holed up here for a few days now while waiting for you."

"That's the kind of romantic idea you can't encapsulate in a short four-line rhyme inside a greeting card," the driver said.

"And that's a good thing," Madeline said.

About twenty yards outside the hanger, the engines on a Gulfstream G600 were already humming, drowning out all other noise.

She took a deep breath and strode toward the office located just inside the hangar. When she opened the door, General Fortner stood and greeted her with a hug and a kiss.

"Are you ready to go?" he asked.

"Yes, I just have to grab my bag from the car," she said.

"We need to go quickly before someone figures out what happened to you," Fortner said.

"But I thought you said everything we were doing would protect me from the truth ever getting out."

Fortner nodded. "And I hope it does, but I don't want to take any chances. That's why it's just you and me tonight flying this bird."

"What?" she asked, her mouth falling agape.

"You heard me."

"But I haven't flown in several years, much less ever captained one of these planes."

Fortner held out his hands in a calming gesture. "You'll be fine. I've flown this plane plenty of times. I'll show you the ropes. Now go get your stuff so we can get going."

Madeline forced a smile as she twirled her silky, brown hair around her finger, a nervous tick she thought she'd left behind in high school. The weight of her decision had already hit, but the real adventure was about to begin. And she couldn't wait to get started.

She strode toward the vehicle and reached inside to grab her bag. The driver handed her a gun.

"You might need this," he said.

"I hope not," she said.

As soon as she slammed the door, the car sped away. She stopped and bit her lip, suppressing a wide grin. Fortner stood at the top of the steps and motioned for her to join him.

"Come on," he yelled. "Let's blow this joint."

She took one step toward the plane when she saw a pair of headlights bouncing along the tarmac and closing fast on her position. She hesitated, unsure of whether she had enough time to make it to the plane before the car arrived.

When the first shot was fired, she didn't hesitate any longer and sprinted back toward the hangar.

CHAPTER 32

HAWK STRAINED TO SEE who the person was standing just outside the hangar, while Black roared toward it. A Gulfstream G600 jet was waiting about thirty yards away from the person's position. Hawk checked his gun and scanned the area once more. There was no backup coming. Blunt had stressed that this situation with the first lady needed to be handled in as quiet of a manner as possible.

As they drew closer, Hawk realized the person was Madeline Young.

"That's her," he said. "Cut her off so she can't reach the plane."

"That was my plan," Black said.

Hawk rolled down his window and fired a warning shot in Madeline's direction. For a moment, he wasn't sure if she would chance a dash toward the jet or retreat to the hangar. After a quick glance back at the jet, she raced inside the hangar's office.

"Get closer before you stop," Hawk instructed.

Black complied and halted their vehicle at an angle, positioning in between the office and the jet. There wasn't a straight shot between them. If she was going to get to the plane, she was going to have to shoot her way through or run around. And Hawk was convinced they could handle either scenario. But there was something he wasn't counting on.

When Hawk stepped out of the car, he was surprised to hear the engines already whirring. He snapped a glance over his shoulder and noticed a man standing just inside the doorway at the top of the steps.

Hawk immediately ducked back inside as a bullet pinged off the car.

"What's the situation?" Black asked as he ducked low.

"It's Fortner. He's already on the plane, and it's ready to leave."

"Damn it. We've put ourselves in a kill box."

"I know," Hawk said. "Why don't you back up a little bit and then you can drive slowly toward the office so I can utilize the car as a cover?"

"Sounds like a plan."

Black threw the car in reverse but kept his head low. Fortner fired two more shots at their vehicle but didn't hit the glass, instead attempting to flatten a tire. Once Black started moving forward again, Hawk slipped outside and walked alongside the car, keeping his head down. After a minute, Black had slowly maneuvered close to the office at an angle that would be more difficult for Fortner to get a clear shot.

Hawk rushed up to the door and kicked it before jumping back. He peered around the corner and noticed it was empty. However, there was a door at the back that was still moving, obviously having just swung open.

Hawk crept back toward the hangar's open space, staying low and using several pallets stacked with supplies and airplane parts as shields.

"Madam First Lady, it doesn't have to end like this," Hawk said. "I'm sure we can work something out for you."

"End like what?" she said from the far corner. "You think you've got me cornered? What are you gonna do? Shoot me?"

Hawk shrugged. "Well, since you're technically already dead, I'm not sure it'd make much of a difference what I did to you now."

"Why don't you disappear now before you're tortured to death?"

"Tortured? Who's going to be torturing me?"

"You don't know these people and what they can do."

"Tell me about them," Hawk said.

He poked his head around the corner of the pallet to see if he could get a better look at where she was. There were workstations and pallets and other aircraft strewn across the open space. He wanted to grab her but couldn't determine a clear path.

When he looked over the top, she fired a bullet at him. Instinctively, he fired back. But instead of burying a shot in her or the building's aluminum siding, he hit a barrel of jet fuel, setting off a big explosion. The heat was so intense that he had to shield his eyes just to see where she was. But it was like she'd vanished.

Hawk was still scanning the hangar for her when Black shouted.

"Over here, Hawk!"

Hawk spun around to see Black on the passenger side of his car, exchanging gunfire with Fortner and Madeline.

What the hell?

Hawk raced over to Black and slid down next to him.

"She came out around the back while you were still talking to her," Black said. "I didn't see her until it was too late. Fortner was laying down cover for her and she came racing around the back side of the building and only had to make it about twenty yards from this angle we have here."

Hawk eased onto his knees to take aim but stopped when he saw Fortner and Madeline working frantically to shut the door.

"They're leaving," Hawk said. "You still got that rifle in the trunk?"

"It's not put together."

"Just give it to me," Hawk said. "We don't have much time."

Black popped the trunk and snatched the rifle case out of it. He slid it back over to Hawk, who went to work assembling the weapon. Meanwhile, the sound emanating from the engines of the Gulfstream G600 intensified as the jet started to move away from them and toward the runway.

"Come on, come on," Black said. "They're speeding away."

"We've got time," Hawk said. "They have to come back by this way."

"You've got a lot of confidence, the kind I'd only have if I was holding an RPG on my shoulder."

Hawk chuckled. "Been there, done that. I guess I needed a new challenge this time."

"So, how exactly is this going to work? Are you going to shoot Fortner through the cockpit glass?"

"Hardly. I'll get maybe two shots to take at the wheels before it won't matter and they'll be going fast enough to get airborne."

"You're going to give the plane a flat tire to keep it grounded?"

"That's the best I could come up with on such short notice," Hawk said.

Hawk got into a prone positioned and eyed the plane. "I hope you got this scoped in recently?"

"I was at the range last week," Black said. "But no guarantees."

"I guess I'll have to make do."

The Gulfstream G600 reached the end of the runway and turned around to begin takeoff. In the distance, the engines roared before the jet lurched forward and sped along the ground. The wheels turned faster as the plane moved closer to Hawk's range.

"Here's goes nothing," he said as he squeezed the trigger. The plane kept charging forward.

"You missed," Black said.

"I've got time for one more shot," Hawk said. He adjusted his scope and took aim.

He exhaled and fired.

This time the bullet struck the front wheel, ripping through the rubber, and shredded the tire. The plane wavered for a moment as Fortner pulled back on the stick to get airborne. However, the airspeed wasn't high enough and the jet dipped to the ground.

Fortner forged ahead even as the front wheel

disintegrated and consisted only of a rim slinging sparks in every direction. When Fortner pulled back on the stick again, gravity wasn't as kind, slamming the plane to the runway. Instead of continuing to roll along, the nose lurched forward as the Gulfstream skidded off the asphalt. Seconds later, the plane burst into flames. Plumes of black smoke were sent skyward, setting off a series of alarms.

"So much for handling this quietly," Black said.

"Let's get out of here," Hawk said. "We don't need our cover blown when the media circus arrives."

CHAPTER 33

BLUNT CRACKED HIS KNUCKLES as he scanned the front page of *The Washington Post*. The headlines blared the news about the shocking attack on the White House and the death of the first lady. Editorials opined about the loss of innocence yet again in America and how the nation as a whole had grown comfortable and let down its guard. Blunt was mildly amused at the tight line some of the president's harshest critics walked, writing how the leader of the free world must be more vigilant for the country's sake yet softening their bitter rhetoric out of respect for the wildly popular first lady.

"How is the president's press secretary spinning that fiasco?" Hawk asked as he walked into the room with Alex and Black.

"He's not," Blunt said as he folded up the paper and tucked it beneath a pile of documents. "Though he'd probably blame us if Young was allowed to acknowledge that we existed."

"You warned him, didn't you?" Alex asked.

Blunt nodded. "He didn't want to believe it at first, but by the time I left, I think his denial had subsided. There was too much smoke for there not to be any fire."

Black shook his head. "What happened after we left Potomac Airfield?"

"Randy Wood sent in a special team to work with the FBI," Blunt said. "The strange thing is they only found one body, and it belonged to General Fortner."

"What's the official position on what happened last night?" Hawk asked. "I'm sure any reporter worth his weight in salt will put two and two together after the bombing and the shady FBI dealings."

"I already thought of that, which is why I gave Camille Youngblood a story about the airplane crash, one that FBI sources verified for her," Blunt said as he reopened his paper. He pointed to an article on the back page of the metro section and slid it across the table to Hawk.

Hawk read the headline aloud. "DEA takes down Columbian drug lord trying to flee U.S."

Alex's eyes widened. "What?"

Hawk read the article for everyone, which detailed how well-known kingpin Hector Diaz was planning on leaving the U.S. with more than seventy-five million in cash in an airplane he'd stolen from

Chile. But federal agents caught him as he tried to leave and shot his airplane, resulting in a catastrophe at the end of the Potomac Airfield runway.

"And Camille just ran with it?" Alex asked.

Blunt nodded and tried to suppress a smile. "It was a win-win situation for the bureau. They needed a plausible excuse for the response to the incident at the airport. And they also needed to explain to the Colombian consulate why Diaz was dead and wouldn't be returning to his homeland. Some agent got a little trigger happy and shot Diaz in the face. A body incinerated in a fire created by jet fuel makes it difficult to assess the cause of death."

"So Madeline Young is still out there?" Black asked.

"Apparently so," Blunt said. "She's been to survival training school and is sufficiently skilled to get out of the country, but she'll need help if she's going to stay hidden. If she resurfaces, that'd be a disaster and a black eye on the face of every federal law enforcement agency."

Black sighed. "What are we gonna do about it?"

"Nothing right now," Blunt said. "We've got other issues to attend to."

"You think Young is going to let us pursue anything else but her when he finds out that she's on the lam?" Alex asked.

"I'll deal with him when that time comes," Blunt said. "He's stable but still in intensive care after nearly dying from smoke inhalation."

"Big Earv is gonna get a medal of honor for saving the president, isn't he?" Hawk asked.

Blunt smiled big and nodded. "Of course he is. And deservedly so in my opinion. That guy is a national treasure in my book."

"So, what next?" Hawk asked. "With no Fortner, we're only left with a name—Falcon Sinclair."

"By the time Alex gets done picking through his dirty laundry, Sinclair is going to wish he was never born," Blunt said as he trimmed the end of his cigar. "We might even use Camille Youngblood to turn the screws on him."

"Whatever it takes," Alex said.

Blunt chewed on his cigar and stared out the window. "Littleton and Joseph may yet provide us with plenty of information, the kind that can help us get a step ahead and be proactive as opposed to a step behind and very reactive."

Blunt's phone buzzed, arresting his attention. He swiped on the screen and read the text message, furrowing his brow as he did.

"What is it?" Alex asked.

"It's from Randy Wood. He said President Young is stable and alert," he said.

Hawk eyed Blunt closely. "That's all it said?"

"No, he asked Wood to pass along a message, requesting that we track down Evana Bahar and bring her to justice."

Black cocked his head to one side. "Evana Bahar? She's not even responsible for this. This feels like 9/11 all over again."

"Is he wrong for wanting that terrorist strung up?" Blunt asked.

Nobody said a word as an awkward silence fell over the room.

"It doesn't matter," Blunt said. "She deserves justice as well. And in the meantime, we can hunt down Sinclair."

"What about Madeline Young?" Alex asked. "Are we just going to let her go free? Two people are dead because of her."

Blunt sighed. "If she becomes a problem, we will. But in the meantime, let's focus on the realized threats instead of the potential ones."

Alex's mouth gaped. "Doesn't the president deserve to know that his wife was a traitor?"

Blunt shrugged. "The real question is this: Would he want to know the truth? I've experienced all levels of betrayal, and trust me when I say this, sometimes it's just better to think a person is dead."

Blunt dismissed the team, leaving him alone in

the conference room with just his thoughts. He paced around the room and considered where his team would go from here. Then he glanced at his phone, which buzzed with another text message, this time from a number he didn't recognize.

He opened the text and dropped the phone almost immediately. It was an image of his niece bound to a chair and screaming for the man with a knife to stop.

"If you'd be so kind to call me back," the note read. "We need you to do us a favor."

Blunt slung his phone against the wall and let out a string of expletives. Obsidian was going to go down in flames, even if it was the last thing he did.

THE END

ACKNOWLEDGMENTS

I am grateful to so many people who have helped with the creation of this project and the entire Brady Hawk series.

Krystal Wade was a big help in editing this book as always.

I would also like to thank my advance reader team for all their input in improving this book along with all the other readers who have enthusiastically embraced the story of Brady Hawk. Stay tuned ... there's more Brady Hawk coming soon.

ABOUT THE AUTHOR

R.J. PATTERSON is an award-winning writer living in southeastern Idaho. He first began his illustrious writing career as a sports journalist, recording his exploits on the soccer fields in England as a young boy. Then when his father told him that people would pay him to watch sports if he would write about what he saw, he went all in. He landed his first writing job at age 15 as a sports writer for a daily newspaper in Orangeburg, S.C. He later attended earned a degree in newspaper journalism from the University of Georgia, where he took a job covering high school sports for the award-winning *Athens Banner-Herald* and *Daily News*.

He later became the sports editor of *The Valdosta Daily Times* before working in the magazine world as an editor and freelance journalist. He has won numerous writing awards, including a national award for his investigative reporting on a sordid tale surrounding an NCAA investigation over the University of Georgia football program.

R.J. enjoys the great outdoors of the Northwest while living there with his wife and four children. He still follows sports closely. He also loves connecting with readers and would love to hear from you. To stay updated about future projects, connect with him over Facebook or on the inter-webs at www.RJPbooks.com and sign up for his newsletter to get deals and updates.

Made in United States
Orlando, FL
27 February 2025

58979407R00171